WORST DAYS

UMBERTO CACCAMO

Paperback: 978-1-968667-47-4
eBook: 978-1-968667-48-1
Library of Congress Control Number: 2025917533

This is a work of fiction.

Ordering Information:

Prime Seven Media
518 Landmann St.
Tomah City, WI 54660

Printed in the United States of America

In Worse Days

THE CHURCH

Once upon a time, in a village not far from our past, a cart with fruit inside was returning from the fields. The high sun beat down on the head of the worker who was walking, after getting off the carriage, pulled by two white horses.

A boy stopped to buy a basket of fruit.

At the side of the road, there was a grocery store with a church opposite, where people were gathered waiting to enter.

The man looked there for a moment, then took a fruit from the cart. Purple fruits.

Asking his owner if he could take some home.

The master didn't know him well; he didn't know his story in depth, but he replied: "Go ahead, you deserved it."

"What did you say your name was?"

"Joseph," the boy replied.

The master stared at him without any premonition about Joseph, as if he was there for a reason which he himself knew deeply.

"Now you have your way on your journey," he added. "The night will watch over you."

Joseph bowed his head, just like that. She feared that there might have been other intentions on his part; she knew that it could be the result of any other provocative act towards her or perhaps witchcraft, as was in vogue at that time. She looked at him, as if she had hit one of his weak spots - he had no family to support. He trembled at the thought of being considered discovered and of losing the little he had managed to procure.

"Bye, Joseph, see you tomorrow."

She looked him straight in the eye and headed home.

He passed by the grocery store on the corner, where his master stopped.

People began to enter the church and noticed the cart on the side of the road; some of them stopped to watch the scene.

It seemed like a normal Sunday in April.

Joseph turned to see what was happening.

He looked at the parked cart, but he didn't quite understand the situation and why people had stopped to look.

A flash of images ran through his mind. He was grateful at that moment, people felt uncomfortable staring into nothingness, as if something was drawing them to pay attention.

He didn't understand exactly what it was about.

Joseph bowed his head, looking at the cart, and noticed nothing.

Someone on the streets heard talk of an imperial carriage that was preparing to pay a visit to the village.

His mind at that moment was clouded with a blue light.

Passing several carriages. He found himself staring into nothingness, his gaze resting on the edge of the road. Passersby, speaking in low voices, passed him by. He remained in a trance–like state with his eyes wide open, not paying attention to them, feeling them as something distant.

He knew he couldn't speak due to the laws regarding magic that were in place at the time, so he narrowed his eyes, as if he understood what was going on.

He indulged without realizing that something was taking root in his mind.

He opened his eyes and lowered his head, feeling as if something had returned to torment his mind with worry.

Her strength, in continuing not to give up, tore him apart. He thought back to the life he had spent before that period, trying to achieve a progress that he himself saw as increasingly distant as the days went by. He lived on lies in order to bring home food. In a continuous state of abandonment.

He knew something was going to change his life any day.

Noon. The sun on the heads of by-passers. Sunday was always a day when people found their moment to take to the streets and engage in confrontations to gain the upper hand.

He found no reason to argue with either his boss or by-passers. So, he knew it was time to go home. Joseph didn't frequent these places much; it was better to go home and prepare something hot. That strange coincidence left him perplexed. A luminescent black carriage, pulled by four white horses, was preparing to approach the church, which stood in the center of the village.

Horse guards were leading him. This scene aroused his interest. He turned his head and stared at the carriage, which stopped a few hundred metres ahead.

The guards got out first. A special atmosphere was created around the carriage. Concern began to spread to all the by-passers, the people who were preparing to spend that Sunday in April as if it were any other Sunday.

The guards quickly dismounted and opened the doors of the carriage, from which first a woman and then a man alighted. Joseph felt something at that moment, a flash struck his mind, a second time, while the people who were looking, petrified at the imperial couple, were irresistibly attracted.

Joseph saw the two come down. A particular harmonious light changed the hierarchies of the people who were present there at that moment. For a moment, the sun disappeared completely, only to reappear a few seconds later much brighter than it had been earlier that Sunday.

Joseph looked up at the sky for a few seconds.

A light penetrated him, a third time that day. He did not understand the importance of supporting it. So, he moved a few meters closer, in the opposite direction from his house. The other people did not understand the reason for the worry that afflicted him at that moment; the prince and the princess were not fully recognised; everyone expected a moment of serenity and tranquility.

But the haste in their faces left Joseph, watching them as if their haste had reminded him of someone, someone he hadn't seen in a long time. He listened to her breathing for a few seconds. He felt as if his thoughts could be heard by someone.

Very slowly, he looked around. The people present didn't pay much attention to him, so he went back to look at what was worrying in their faces. The imperial couple came down, looking around with an air of mystery and concern. They headed into the church.

Nothing special happened immediately, but the sensation that was felt at that moment made the mouths of by-passers palpitate and caused a few moments of unease.

Joseph kept staring at them, taking in every detail as if something caught his attention as he observed their behavior. Some children passed by him.

They screamed with happiness and did not understand the concern that the adults felt.

He turned his head and noticed a person who was standing next to him and who was watching in amazement, like many others at that moment.

"Do you know what happened?"

She was a nobly dressed woman, with a typical dress of that period, very colorful, she had pearly eyes and red hair.

He was suddenly amazed.

He turned his attention back to the carriage.

The woman looked away for a moment and replied:

"Something in the forest it put out a flash last night. Nothing was found, the guards headed there without finding an answer."

Joseph was scared for a moment, he suddenly opened his eyes and turned away so as not to attract attention.

At that time, magic was not known as something dangerous. Not everyone had the power to know its foundations.

Joseph trembled with fear, as if something was pressing on his head, preventing him from focusing on his situation properly.

She turned away for a moment, as if to think back to the flash that had seen her petrify at first that day.

He bowed his head toward the woman, asking where it came from, why the concern on their faces was so suddenly marked by their haste, and who was interested in hearing the message they had to convey.

He didn't realize it at the time, but his hand began to shake just before his question.

The woman did not seem impressed. For a moment, she stared at the hand then looked at him with her angelic face, it was as if she already knew such a question would be asked by him.

He turned around, his eyes continuing to observe what had happened. She turned her gaze towards him for a second moment.

"Paths in the dark always lead to roads."

Suddenly, Joseph looked away and for a moment he didn't answer, he thought he wanted to run away and go home. But he knew that in this way he would attract the attention of the mysterious woman and the people around him. He turned sharply, as if to hide his gaze and get to safety. The woman disappeared. He turned around to see if anyone had noticed what his eyes had seen at that moment. His thoughts returned to the carriage, to the people, to his life and to the questions that at that moment clouded his mind. His particular awareness that made him alone in that moment, after so much journey, to find himself the only one with the certainty of what he had experienced up to that moment.

No one observed his thoughts or could even imagine what his mind was trying to tell him at that moment.

She often counted on Gressy, on the people she saw lost on her way there, it worries her that she accepted a natural conception of where she was at that moment. What would get her there?

He asked himself many times, often. In his memory, there was only the awareness of a previous world that he forgot about himself.

Her eyes were wide open, and for a moment she turned very slowly as the imperial couple walked out of the church. He covered his face with a feeling of unease, which he had never felt before.

Joseph was only twenty years old. As young as he was as a boy at his age, he always had the thought of his parents' discomfort, abandoned when he was just six months old. He had a clear memory of the moment his parents abandoned him.

That sense of loneliness heightened the perception of that memory that resurfaced in him, reminding him of his true nature of who he really was. Experiencing a state of abandonment and the cruel fate to which he had been destined.

He didn't look back to see what would happen after the two left the church.

The carriage horses neighed; their hooves clattered along the streets, and the wheels began their march. People began to wonder quietly again what was going to happen.

On the way home, people continued to talk in very low tones about what had happened. Joseph, with his head halfway up, continued without looking at anyone. He had a feeling that someone might have heard him conversing with the mysterious woman who had disappeared so suddenly.

Joseph found his strength to return home.

After all, that Sunday in April had left him with a sense of revenge for his frustration: he knew that what he had brought home was much more necessary than it should be. Within the walls of the place where he lived, he felt safe, even if the thrill of that day returned several times to question him. After so many years, he managed to begin what for him might have been lost in his reminiscence of remembering who he really was.

The fire was lit, the embers were fogging up, almost disappearing under the ashes. He placed the little he had earned on the table, and he would consume a few bites, just to silence his hunger.

Unusually, he had left the door ajar without realizing it.

He put some wood on fire.

The night was cold; the fire had been burning since the night before. He filled the teapot with water that had been stagnant in the bucket.

He took off the boots he had been wearing all morning. He took off his clothes and went to bed. He needed to rest.

More days of incessant, non-stop travel awaited him. He would walk for days without looking back, following the direction that came to him. His route had been indicated to him before his departure.

The godmother who had welcomed him, named Gressy, had revealed to him the particular reasons why his path was one of the most difficult to follow and to be considered as a solution. It crossed mountains, rivers, and lakes. Facing illnesses that he could not distinguish himself from, finding himself confronted with the harsh art of survival. He carried with him a shoulder bag made from the skin of a strange animal that had not been seen for years, the only object that his godmother had given him, along with a few provisions, now rotten inside the bag, degrading with the passing of time. She explained to him how to follow the birds; she knew they would take him there.

THE ROAD

Gres or Gres, that's what he called himself.

I had been cared for by an elderly couple who I had thought were my parents. They never told me the story of how I came to be in their family or why they had welcomed me during my childhood. Theirs was a very sad story. Gressy is killing me. One day he came to pick me up. I never saw them again. They didn't even look out, I didn't turn back to look at them, it was my last memory. They were simple people: the old man remembered, worked the wood, the old lady took care of the house and prepared hot meals for when it was lunch time. They never told me where they came from. No story to tell, no sign of particular attachment, no other way to remember what had brought me there. They kept all these things from me all this time and asked me to let it go.

I remember spending a lot of time observing the anthills and wondering how the ants' homes were built; I tried to imagine what it might have been like inside. The old woman, who had a peculiar name I don't remember, called me when I'd stare at the edge of the stream playing with the ants, which I often remember as the stream water swelled and washed them away.

"Joseph! What are you doing? Hurry, it's almost ready. And stop looking at those ants."

I was about seven or eight years old, and my memories weren't very clear. I was mostly trying to remember why they'd brought me to their house.

The old man made pipes all day. Once he had me trim a piece of wood and make an arrow out of it. They mostly earned their living from the pipes he made and supported themselves just outside the village where they lived.

Gressy, I remember, took me out of there with her. She didn't tell me much about them, but that they had taken the time to spend with me. That was enough to convince me that they would pass by without me ever seeing them again. I didn't even have time to ask her or show any sign of interest with many words.

I didn't bring anything with me; I wore simple shorts and a jacket that kept me warm. After a few days of walking with the carriage, we reached the village. The weather there was much warmer than up north.

We arrived at Gressy's house. It was outside the town and looked half-destroyed: anyone looking at it would have guessed that no one lived there. She immediately introduced me to her sons, Victor, five, and Vincent, eight.

After days of walking by carriage, we arrived at the village.

For days, my loneliness was unrelieved. The feeling that carried me away from the old people's house. It brought the expression of a memory of mine into a solitude far from that house, which was gradually receding.

For the first time, I found myself alone, but with people my own age. And one of them, whom I called Mom, seemed younger than the mom I was used to.

Gressy asked her eldest son to show me the bed.

I first met five-year-old Victor, who showed me his bed without introducing himself. We sat down, and I asked if we could look out onto the street.

Victor replied, "Yes, just a moment, it's almost lunchtime. Mommy doesn't want to."

Vincent arrived shortly after; he had a dominant personality, spoke much more than Victor and paid little attention to his brother. He introduced himself immediately; from the first moment he saw me, he made sure to focus on every interest.

Victor looked at me jealously, with a face that seemed regretful, but he showed no emotion and was unresponsive.

Meanwhile, Gressy called us to the table. We left the room. As we reached the table, her companion joined us. He looked serene, as if he already knew he'd find something new at home.

He already knew my name. Gressy had most likely mentioned it to him a few days earlier.

"Hi, Joseph," he said, "I'm Steph. Welcome home."

We sat down and Gressy served us a hot meal. For the first time, I was amazed at how carefully the table was laid out and how clean and tidy it was.

In the old people's hut, Grandma sat by the fire and the old man ate on the bed.

Gressy sat next to Steph; there wasn't much conversation at first.

Steph looked at me and asked how I had traveled and how I had found the house once inside. And touching Victor, she asked, "You have met these two beasts, right?"

Gressy looked at me for a moment and then looked at Vincent, a sign of understanding.

Steph asked Gressy, "Did the merchant give you the money he owed you?"

Gressy replied, "No, not yet. Do you have any news?"

"The research leader told me it's not time yet, it takes a little patience, I think I still need to find some more iron."

"And the money? Where do we get it?" the woman asked.

"You know, maybe I'll go with the search party; they need a few more men for the hunt."

"Look, we can't risk everything."

Gressy looked at Victor for a moment, then fixed his gaze on Steph.

Meanwhile, I was incredulous at hearing such conversations; I had no idea what they meant. I'd never heard anyone talk like this at the table before.

"Do you understand?" Gressy asked, turning to Steph.

"It's lunchtime, that's enough for now," she replied.

For the first time, I knew what it meant to be at the table. I learned this thanks to Gressy. She was a very lively woman, not much interested in paying attention to us children, much less in stepping aside and being a housewife.

I discovered another reality; I hadn't quite figured out the name of the village, and I hadn't yet set foot on the new land I would learn to call home again.

The next morning Steph left, and there was no way to say goodbye. I would know, like a loud noise, when he'd be back.

I woke up with a groggy, full head, as if I'd had a thousand conversations. I rarely spoke. I hadn't left the house yet. The new village gave me a sense of disarray; I felt disoriented. I got out of bed and went outside to see where Gressy, Victor, and Vincent were. So, I tested the new air. Outside, I found Vincent, who greeted me with a half-smile. "Come on, I was waiting for you to buy some things Mom asked me for down at the market." I didn't hesitate; I watched Victor play with a piece of wood and dig little grooves that looked like riverbeds.

Vincent grabbed his brother.

"Come on, let's go. I always have to call you back.

Let's go, Joseph."

We crossed a street that ran around the corner of the house, and we continued to the right and then immediately left.

On the street, people were carrying what they had. As we turned left, on the right I saw a series of tables like the ones in the kitchen. People were placing food on them. It was something unusual, something I'd never seen before. The elders had never even mentioned it, nor did they take me to see what was in the village where I grew up.

Victor asked me, "What's so strange that you're staring in amazement at those tables?"

There was everything, from fruit to some gray stick-like objects I'd never seen before. A stone with two holes in its sides from which water flowed was placed in the center of the square. On it were candles. Two of them were unlit.

I asked Vincent what it was.

He replied, "Have you never seen anything like it?"

I shook my head, nodding. The only thing I'd seen full of it was the stream.

Vincent asked me to wait there with Vincent, while I stared in amazement at the candles, with water pouring out of the holes in the sides. For a moment, I looked up and heard a noise that frightened me. I squinted my eyes and face.

It came from a large house.

"Vincent, what is that?"

Vincent, walking toward me with a rag in his hand, came toward me.

He pointed to the large, noisy building. He nodded and said, snorting, "It's a church. Haven't you ever seen anything like that?"

"No. Why that noise?"

Looking at me, he immediately realized I wasn't lying and added, "Have you never seen a church?! Have you never been inside one?"

"Can we go?" I asked.

"Today isn't Sunday! I'll take you there another day."

"Victor," said Vincent, "come on, you don't want to wash your face all day."

I looked at that place in disbelief before leaving. We started walking home and, even before taking a step to go, Vincent handed me the things he had bought at the market, or rather on the tables.

I'd realized the large, noisy building was called "Church," I repeated to myself.

Looking down, I found Vincent standing before me.

"What are you waiting for? Here, this is yours."

He handed me the piece of cloth, and I opened it. Inside was something that looked like a piece of wood, I thought, and one of those fruits the old people told me not to eat.

"Vincent, what do I owe you with the wood?"

"Bread, it's called bread. Mom told me to look at Victor, not you."

"Can we eat it?"

Vincent looked at me as we walked toward home. He didn't immediately answer the question. I looked up, then down, and looked again at the piece of wood, which from that day on I would call bread. Holding it in my hand, I observed and admired it closely. I sniffed it several times, and keeping my head down, I took three steps, colliding with a man standing a few meters from the stone. He spread his arms, frightened, letting go of what he was holding.

Looking at the stranger, I said, "I, I didn't mean to."

The man replied,

"Are you okay, boy?"

"YES," I replied.

He picked up the fruit with the bread, wrapped it in the cloth, and said to me, "Keep your head up, boy." The man was wearing green clothes with dark pants and some chopsticks he kept in a bottle.

I ran to catch up with Vincent. I turned and looked back as if to thank him. For a couple of seconds, I had spoken to someone I didn't know; I was so ashamed that I scared myself, but at the same time, it was as if I was rejoicing inside. For a moment, our eyes met.

I reached Vincent, scared and breathing hard, placing my hands on my knees.

"Who was that?"

"He's a village guard," he replied.

Vincent turned his head toward Victor and said, "I lost you a minute and you're already in trouble."

"What?" He exclaimed, "a guard?" And as I looked at him suspiciously, strange sensations flashed through my mind for a moment. My heart was pounding; I didn't know if they were emotions or something that needed to be avoided.

Vincent looked at me with a tired expression and said, "It's your second day here and I still don't understand you."

Yesterday you didn't speak, and today I almost have to hold your hand to get out of the cash register. You're the same age as me.

"Let's go, Joseph!"

We walked the same route we'd taken to the market. Vincent continued walking home as if nothing had happened, never looking at me, to hide his embarrassment. Was it possible that the old folks had never taken me somewhere like this, and that there wasn't a market in the village where I could buy something to eat?

They arrived home, but Gressy hadn't returned. Vincent and Joseph sat on the kitchen chairs. Joseph didn't ask anything, just stared at the door, while Victor went out to play with his stick, which he then left on the windowsill.

Vincent went outside and sent his brother to get a bucket of water. Meanwhile, lunchtime had arrived, but Gressy hadn't returned.

Joseph was the first to retreat to his room, lay down on the bed, closed his eyes for a moment, and fell asleep.

When he awoke, he realized he'd slept a little longer than usual. He was so tired he hadn't even realized he'd slept so much.

Vincent and Victor remained awake. Gressy was distraught and had gone to Joseph's room.

It was almost sunset. The boy awoke to find the woman on the windowsill. For a moment, he stared at one spot, reflecting on what had happened to him that morning.

Gressy noticed he looked shaken and called out to him:

"Joseph, are you okay?"

Joseph nodded.

Gressy knew something was wrong; she had sensed that sense of frustration in him, something she knew well.

She bowed her head for a moment, so Joseph couldn't see it.

"Are you hungry?" Gressy asked.

"Let's go over there, I brought something, come on."

Joseph felt pain, as if something had hit him. As he stood up, it suddenly disappeared.

He looked at himself and touched his body more slowly than usual. He went to Gressy, who handed him some water.

"Another piece of wood?" Joseph asked.

Gressy looked at him in amazement, glancing at Vincent and Victor.

"What do you mean, a piece of wood? Did you guys fight?"

Vincent, fed up and rolling his eyes, said

"Yes, first the bread, now the meat."

Gressy flashed a smile and quickly turned away, so as not to embarrass Joseph.

Then she asked Vincent, "Didn't you tell him about magic wands? You know, those things haven't existed for years or decades."

Victor looked at Gressy, not noticing Joseph trying to understand and test the meat in his hands. He asked Gressy, "Why is the church called a big, noisy thing?"

Gressy turned to Victor: "Why so noisy? Where were you all this morning?"

Joseph replied: "With the guards at the tables." Gressy shouted to get Vincent's attention. "Vincent!"

Vincent looked at Joseph as if he had something to hide, not to embarrass him. Gressy looked at Vincent in shock and rebuked him: "I told you the three of you shouldn't have gone there."

"Stone, stone!" Victor exclaimed.

"Okay, Mom, next time I won't bring him to the tables," she replied, looking disgustedly at Victor.

Gressy returned to her things and in the meantime sent Vincent out to get some wood; she knew she couldn't send Victor out there. So she prepared the teapot, poured some water into it, and placed it on the fire.

She turned to the table to watch Joseph, whom she had seen leave moments earlier, carrying the dried meat she had brought him.

It was the first time Joseph saw so many things he didn't know existed.

Before, he had never come across tables with gray sticks holding fruit and food. His eyes sparkled again as if by magic, intensely with someone he had never met. Back in bed, he touched the edges of his eyes with the tips of his hands; he had no idea what it meant to touch his face like that. Out of shame, he hid, waiting for his brothers to arrive.

In those days, Steph set out with the search party, heading into the forest.

They began a new mission, aiming to find supplies. The group's leader planned the search north of the village, in the mountains. They set out in the morning, with only the moonlight and torches lit, one for every three people.

They usually had two groups of twelve, one heading into the forest to the northeast and the other to the northwest. Steph was the weapons maintainer, mostly for hunting. He made axes, spearheads, and arrowheads—everything involving wrought iron. They set out on foot with supplies that would last them for a few days. It wasn't Steph's first time; he had been on several expeditions with the search party.

He had begun his service a few years earlier, to better manage supplies and ensure he could rely on what he built. The commander's name was Gilbert.

He was a tall, lanky man with funny hair, very fussy, and possessed a sense of revenge that drove him to brag every chance he got. His attitude was well known, and the boys who were with him weren't surprised, but they knew that when he conquered something, he usually attracted the others' attention.

Steph wasn't well-liked by the commander, as he knew he had to keep a close eye on the type of equipment he provided for the group. It didn't really matter; he didn't carry any actual weapons with him; he had spare parts to use if something went wrong.

Only fifteen of them set out. The group walked for several hours before reaching the foot of the mountain, behind which lay a dense, flat forest. Its borders, marked by the people who had founded the village, had a dark side. No one had attempted to cross them since. People didn't speak much; there was a great sense of privacy and respect for that forest. Of the fate of the forest, no one spoke of what happened. None of those who advanced to combat what had once threatened the village spoke of missing persons or disasters of any kind. The ancients insisted that Ono never venture beyond the limits that had been imposed.

Steph, the commander, and the rest of the group set off, carrying only the few supplies each had with them. The search party had no reason to stay out for long.

The commander was the only one dressed in a gleaming beige outfit and a hat with a feather on his head. No one understood what that bizarre hat could mean. The rest of the expedition wore dark pants and green jackets. Some of them stood out because of the strange animal skins they wore.

The group, led by the commander, reached the entrance to the forest. Trees were beginning to rise around them, far apart from each other, wondering if someone had decided to plant them there. They glimpsed the first sign.

Steph said to the commander, "We stopped."

"Yes," Gilbert replied. "Do you remember anything, or did you just forget overnight?"

Steph looked at the group in bewilderment. Despite his role in the village and the service he provided to the group and the guards, he couldn't hear very well and had memory lapses that caused him to forget things and not remember clearly.

Steph lowered her gaze, briefly placed her left hand on her head, and touched her fingers near her eyes.

"This is the first sign," the commander explained. "There will be others. A sign very different from the others will indicate the point from which we can hunt."

They usually hunted birds, other animals that over the years were becoming increasingly lost in the forest. They had the strange sensation of being watched, although none of them could explain where it came from. Very often, the eyes lead where the mind doesn't want. From the outside, all you know is the sensation of having nothing in front of you.

New recruits were joining the group. Some of them often joked, muttering to other companions.

The group stopped in a circle. The companion turned for a moment to the new recruit, asking,

"Today is your first day, isn't that right?"

Gilbert began to explain,

"You know, these stones weren't placed that way by our ancestors. We don't know their true nature, and we don't know where they came from or what kind of rock they're made of."

Then he turned toward the mountain and gave the order to begin marching.

He stopped just as the group set off again.

Turning to the recruit,

"Three heads? It gets worse! Those are just birds."

They continued at a slow pace, there was no rush to return to the village.

The only people who knew about those blocks were the ancestors. No one ever understood the purpose of leaving those markings on the ground, nor was there any mention of them in the village. Steph walked a few meters behind the group, still rubbing the back of her neck, often reaching the height of her left eyebrow. She stared at the hand for a moment, which briefly caught her attention. Then she looked and quickened her pace for a couple of meters.

Gressy waited a few moments before going to bed. She realized the children were asleep, so she sat down for a moment by the fire. The season there was completely different from what Joseph remembered; they marched for a couple of days before reaching the village south of Joseph's childhood home.

During the day, it was pleasant; the sun, high above the ground, after lunchtime, began to set behind the mountain that loomed north of the village. The temperature dropped significantly, a chilly air reaching the lower parts of the stomach, and it felt as if something were beginning to enter people's bodies.

It was the same for Gressy. People, however, didn't notice because they had become accustomed to it long ago. No one really knew why the weather rarely changed. During the growing season, self-supporting bushes would sprout, growing a couple of meters tall. The fruit had a strange greenish color verging on yellow. For tea, they used wild plants and a strange flower as big as a man's hand, white, usually with five petals. For the meat, they followed a process that was explained to me, known only to a few ancient people. I learned so much in such a short time that it filled my mind; the strange season and everything that was new to me filled part of that imagination that saw me projected as if into the house of ants.

Even Gressy didn't know much about how things were formed; for tea was extracted from plants whose nature was unknown. The plants grew spontaneously, without planting any seeds, partly because everyone was unaware of the nature of the seed and how those plants could grow in such strange shapes and different colors, an unnatural form.

In the village, there were places where people drank a strange green beverage that temporarily altered the senses but lowered their mood. This was extracted from a bud and added to a solution of water and some red berries that the research team usually carried with them in small quantities. From that bright color, poured into wooden cups, they lit up like small lanterns.

Gressy sat by the fire staring into the flame and occasionally turning towards Joseph's room behind her.

Gressy realized it was her instinct calling his attention. It could be a sign. She was a woman who didn't talk much about her inner self-knowledge, for fear of saying what might seem completely unusual and unreasonable to others.

She sipped the remaining tea, its warmth no longer emitting. Her body had adjusted. She moved away from the fire and walked toward the door.

She saw on the sideboard some objects rolled up in cloth that the old people had left for Joseph. She didn't particularly notice, but went to the windowsill and took a breath of fresh air. She stared into the darkness for a few seconds, keeping the door ajar, then turned to look inside, closed the door, and secured it with a piece of wood that fit into the left side of the frame. Only the firelight illuminated the table and the other objects. She went to her room and, sighing several times, got into bed; He stared at the ceiling for a few minutes with teary eyes, turned onto his side and fell asleep.

The search party advanced through the forest; the sun was setting much earlier than expected, and Steph was beginning to remember that it had always been this way when he'd been there. The feeling of not having the sunlight to guide him was faint. He feared the dark. His mind knew deeply what had happened to him and helped him remember the moments spent there. The good dose of instinct Steph sensed spoke to him, protecting him and showing him the way, so much so that he wasn't following what he wanted, but instinct that led him along the path. He turned back for a moment to see how far they had gone. He glimpsed the first signs of the new night light, which at first glance looked like a luminescent white arc glowing like daylight.

Then he turned to the commander, who was marching with the group following.

"Gilbert, oh, excuse me, Commander. We'd better stop; in the darkness, we won't be able to get our bearings."

The commander had heard someone say something to him, so he paused for a moment to turn toward the rest of the group, not immediately sure who it was.

Gilbert asked, "Who spoke?"

"Commander!"

For a few seconds, Gilbert didn't recognize his voice, but as the rest of the group continued on, he took two steps closer to Steph, who was falling into line behind them.

"Steph, did you say something?"

Steph didn't answer at first; he knew he had to be careful not to say something he shouldn't have said.

So, he answered: "The light. In the night, we don't know our way."

The commander looked at him for a few seconds, sighing.

Steph, there's nothing to worry about, we'll be stopping soon. You strike your sword while I think about where to go. You look more agitated than expected."

Steph only understood the last sentence and lowered her gaze. The commander realized that she didn't trust her thoughts very much; her mind was decidedly less clear than the others.

Steph didn't answer and immediately looked straight ahead, avoiding the commander's gaze as he tried to clarify his position.

The rest of the group continued for a few meters, and someone exclaimed:

"Commander, we found something."

"What are they?"

Another member of the group added, as everyone crowded together to take a closer look at their discovery, driven by curiosity.

Those who knew already knew what it was all about.

The commander turned to the rest of the group, as they approached with curiosity.

The commander preceded them, stopping them, hurried ahead of them, and made his way through the boys.

"Stop! Let me pass." Arriving in front of that strange shrub, Gilbert froze.

It was a unique shrub, which attracted the attention of the new recruits.

The boys kept wondering what they were. When the commander looked at the plant, he had never seen one so close to the edge of the forest. He knew he still had a few days' walk to go, so he said to himself, "It shouldn't be here, so far from where they're supposed to be."

The questions he was asking had no concrete answers. Looking at them with an incredulous expression, he said to the boys,

"Pick them, but don't eat them right away. Once picked, they must change color before they're edible."

The new recruit turned to the commander, delighted with the discovery.

"What are they called? What are they called?"

"They're berries," Gilbert replied, "the ones used in the drink you drink in the grocery store."

The commander turned for a moment and looked at Steph, who, unlike the rest of the group, showed no interest in the plant. He bowed his head.

"Take them, we'll need them for a few days."

The commander sighed for a few seconds, slowly touching his head with his hand.

One of the boys approached him.

"Commander, why are you there?"

Gilbert remained lost in thought, his mind searching for an explanation.

He turned, looking at his companion.

"Rod," he said.

We passed by here a while ago and there wasn't a trace of these bushes. Why are they here now? What are you thinking?" the boy asked.

The commander stood still and turned to him. For a moment, Rod had the impression that I was showing him that I was afraid of something.

"Rod, get the supplies, everything's fine, there's nothing to worry about," Gilbert said, but immediately shook his head, as if to get a move on and not let him know he was lying.

Rod had realized that there was something about the berries that worried him, but it certainly had nothing to do with the changing earth.

The boy nodded. "Tell the others we'll stop here for the night," the man ordered, before walking away.

"Let's camp here tonight. Get some firewood. It'll be better if we're not left alone in the night sun."

Rod pushed all doubts from his mind, any other suspicion.

He hadn't seen the commander behave like that. The boys took off their packs and put their weapons on the ground. The chill air began to make itself felt, the daylight began to take on a dark hue south of the village.

A strange terror began to grow in the commander's mind.

Steph stared into space for a long time. He wasn't looking for answers. He approached the plant the boys had seen. Amazed, he noticed that it had colorful leaves. That plant was surviving and had been able to adapt. Steph knelt down.

He picked up a leaf and examined it closely, turning it over in his hands several times.

He moved a few meters behind the bush and saw a tree behind him, to the left. He took a few steps, but an unpleasant sensation twisted his stomach for a few seconds. Perhaps it had something to do with what the commander had thought.

He looked at the tree for a few seconds and noticed another plant at its base; it was starting to grow. It had a few white flowers, but he didn't quite recognize it.

He bent down to observe the structure of the flower and saw a strange shrub below that had an unusual yellowish color. It had a trunk, unlike that of the tree, smaller in size, and a strange bell-shaped cap. He picked it up, but for a moment he paused as he picked it up. He wondered if he was doing the right thing. He took one of his arrowheads and pulled it from the ground. He stared for a moment at the plant beside him. He began to doubt what it was. He stood up. But as he rose, the strange fruit hit the branch of the plant and broke. He picked up the other piece. He didn't notice that the fruit had changed color in the meantime. It turned a deep blue.

He was frightened and dropped it. He took a step back, shocked by what had happened. He looked around, hoping he hadn't attracted the others' attention. The rest of the group was busy getting ready for the night.

He looked at the fruit again. He realized something was wrong; his left hand began to tremble.

He felt a sharp pain in his head, which he didn't recognize as anything else. The mushroom drew him there for some reason.

Meanwhile, the commander, who had moved a few meters away, had returned to the camp and asked Rod, "Have you seen Steph?"

Rod, without looking at the commander, said in a low tone, "I don't know." He turned and returned to his things. He put the axe back on the ground without looking where he'd put it.

The commander turned to the rest of the group and asked, "Have you seen Steph?"

Without moving, he looked back at Rod, who replied,

"She'll be around."

Someone added, "No."

"No one?" the commander insisted.

"I'm here, commander," Steph intervened.

"I was just a second away."

The commander saw him emerge from behind the tree.

He wasn't used to talking to Steph. After several expeditions in the past, Steph knew the commander well. He paid attention to him, unless he had a specific request that belonged to him. Steph stopped at the tree, hid what he had found, trying not to show off what he was holding with too many gestures.

The commander approached and asked,

"Tonight, the two of us will take guard duty, okay?"

Steph had never held such a duty, especially since she had never held a weapon in her hand. She didn't answer immediately, but after a few moments she agreed.

"All right," said Steph.

"You look strange," observed Gilbert.

The commander didn't wait for a response but went on to give further instructions.

"I'll stay awake until the others go to sleep.

You and Rod will stand guard after I wake you. What's that in your hand?" he asked, pointing to it.

He suddenly turned to the boys.

"You go and fix the fire. The night here will be harsh, not like in the village. Hurry up. What are those faces?!"

Steph settled herself next to the tree next to her. She realized she couldn't speak, so she set her things down. She sat down with her back against the trunk. She picked up some meat and chewed a bit, looking at her hand.

"The hand," she repeated softly.

"The hand."

He raised his head for a moment and rested it against the tree trunk.

Meanwhile, the commander directed the group.

"You don't want to catch some disease, do you? There are some things you've never seen before.

Find a way to stay out in the cold."

Rod looked at Gilbert and, for a moment, at the rest of his companions; he feared those words were not a good omen.

The commander moved a few meters outside, dropped his bag and his hunting weapons.

No one had quite understood what he had said.

Gilbert sat down and rummaged through his bag, keeping an eye on the rest of the group. He began to rummage slowly through the bag, wondering if he was doing the right thing, pausing for a moment.

He went back to rummaging through the bag. He first removed some food wrapped in a piece of cloth, then a strange piece of wood used to call birds, and was about to reach for another object when a new recruit called out to him.

"Commander, commander!"

Gilbert jerked and put everything back in his bag so as not to be seen, and looked up slowly so as not to arouse the boy's suspicions.

"Yes?"

"We've prepared something hot. Would you like to join us?"

The commander remained completely indifferent, his face seemingly impassive even though he felt a tremor inside him that he had never felt before. The new recruit stared at him for a few seconds, then turned to the rest of the group to understand what had happened.

The commander, petrified,

"I'm coming. Give me a few moments to get my things ready."

The new recruit replied, "We'll wait for you, Commander."

No one welcomed the commander, who, with a few sighs, continued to rummage through his bag. He took a piece of meat and freed it from the cloth it was wrapped in. He paused for a moment, looking up. He took a bite. His mind was catapulted back into his past.

He listened to his breathing again.

He continued to look at the forest that appeared before him, observing it, seeing the trees that spread thickly at the foot of the mountain. Chewing the piece of meat he held in his hand, the past blossomed again. He slumped and hunched his shoulders, observing the landscape illuminated by the night's sunlight.

Steph fell asleep and didn't wake up to the sound of the boys chatting and shouting in euphoria, "Did you see what I found?"

"If it weren't for me, we wouldn't have found any supplies."

"Stop it, don't make a fuss, let's not lose our minds. Did you hear what the commander said?"

One of the new recruits replied,

"The worry disappeared years ago, my grandfather always told me that."

"Keep your eyes open, we're not here to laugh and joke."

Another new recruit replied, "You can save that worry for when I find something better."

For a moment, Steph opened his eyes and looked at the commander and the boys. He lowered his head to his right to search for his bag with his right hand, rummaging through it.

He was so tired that it felt like he'd been working with his mind all day, even during the little time he'd slept. He found the fruit, touched it, and let his head fall to one side, going back to sleep.

Rod. He took a few steps to the right, from where the boys had camped, and walked away for a while; he was looking for a stream he remembered nearby. The sky was turning blue; in the night sunlight, the trees could be seen, glowing white on one side.

The camp was now behind him. Without realizing it, Rod had wandered much further than he should have. He looked back to get his bearings.

A few hundred meters ahead, he found some berry plants. He knelt down to pick them up and put them in his bag. He looked up for a moment, as if something had caught his attention.

He stared at a point beyond some bushes.

He knew he could continue no further in that solitary search in the night.

Rod knew part of the forest, he knew what had happened there in the previous years. His eyes had seen what perhaps few knew, and what had remained in the minds of the people who had survived in the village. He, along with other members of the search party, remember what had been unleashed in the past. At that time, his search party took another route. They split into two groups, one taking the forest to the east and the other to the west. The other search party had to face those ferocious monsters that moved in the night for a long time; for weeks on end, they were thought to be missing. Rod and Gilbert returned prematurely from that long expedition in the forest. The second group, which went west, did not return in the expected time, and few survived.

Rod did not join the search party in the following years. The constant checks that followed forced him to spend time alone, unlike Gilbert, who continued to train the group.

Rod had realized that something had changed during the time that had passed: the stream was still in the same place, nor could he hear the water rustling on the stones. The source came from the forest. There were many more plants than expected. Plants that only grew at a certain height.

He quickened his pace to reach the stream. He pushed through the vegetation that covered his legs to half his torso. He found the stream. He was surprised to see plants with white, five-petalled flowers growing on the bank.

He bent down, washed his face with his hands, and then sipped some water to quench his thirst. He gazed at the flowers, incredulous. He admired their beauty; they shone in the light: white, like stamens sprouting purple. He reached out to pick a few. With his other hand, he brought the bag at his side forward. He opened it and placed them in the bag. He quickly stood up and returned to the camp.

THE CORSAIR

Long ago, before the formation of the research corps, half the village's inhabitants lived there. Rod and Gilbert were young and didn't know each other. Gilbert's father farmed the land, while his mother took care of the clothes and prepared meals for Gilbert and his sister. Rod was a few years younger. There weren't many houses in the village. There was no market square; instead of a fountain, there was a well. A simple well, with a bucket and a rope surrounded by a circle of stones. The well often filled with rainwater. The seasons were different back then. Days lasted much longer than nights, but in winter, night took up much of the day. Gilbert's father farmed the land and used what he harvested to feed the villagers. He took what little he had left home. In return, the other villagers lent a hand when needed, or when Gilbert's father needed it. His wife helped the older people by embroidering and sewing clothes, mending shoes, and, if necessary, preparing something warm. Gilbert tended the wood. He often walked alone to the foot of the mountain, sometimes with his sister Siby to keep him company. Gilbert was nine, his sister five. They often misunderstood each other. He always scolded his sister, because of her personality. Siby had brown hair and brown eyes. Gilbert often looked at them in amazement. His sister played with whatever she found and was often spellbound by the lake.

It wasn't far from the village; you could glimpse it from the window of the house.

Gilbert spent a lot of time looking out the windowsill; he loved watching the different types of flocks migrate to the lake.

One day, he and Siby had an argument. They returned home after gathering firewood. Gilbert threw the firewood on the ground before returning.

Siby came into the house shouting, "Mommy, have you seen the firewood? Now I can go play in the lake!"

It was almost dark, the light was fading.

Meanwhile, Gilbert had reached the lake and started throwing stones.

Mommy looked at Siby, then turned her head toward the window, saying, "It's almost dark. Daddy will be home soon."

The little girl became furious, lowering her head slightly, her eyebrows narrowing, and her eyes bulging as she glared at her mother.

The woman insisted.

"It's almost dark, there's no one outside."

Siby continued to stare at her and protested.

"Gilbert's gone, why do I have to stay home?"

With a sigh, she turned again and opened a drawer, reaching inside and replying.

"Okay."

She waited a few seconds before stopping Siby, who was coming out the front door.

"Wait! Bring this." Siby took what her mother had given her without looking; she put it in the pocket of her long dress, turned, and ran out of the house. Gilbert was already tired of throwing stones and sat on the lake shore, staring at the water, throwing a few stones every now and then. Siby was coming, and she couldn't help but be happy to throw a few stones. She crossed one path and then skipped another.

Her shoes were all holes. She tripped over a small bush. She fell chest-first into the pooling water in the grass, which was almost taller than her. She immediately got up and joined her brother.

"Hey, Gilbert! Did you see? I made it this far, too."

Gilbert remained impassive.

Siby stopped and looked at the lake for a moment.

"Now I can throw some pebbles, too."

Gilbert hadn't noticed her, and when he heard her speak, he turned in disbelief and burst out laughing. Siby stood for a second watching Gilbert hold his stomach in his arms, then bent down to look for some pebbles. Gilbert looked at her again.

"Where have you been? And why are you looking like this?"

Siby approached the edge of the lake, a pebble in her hand. She threw it a few feet away, put her hand in her pocket, and turning to Gilbert, said,

"Look. Mommy gave me something."

He turned and looked at Siby's hand, which was rummaging in the pocket of her knee-length dress. Gilbert couldn't tear his attention away; he was particularly drawn to what Siby wanted him to see. Siby took her hand out of her pocket and opened it. In her palm was a piece of faded yellow metal with a five-petaled flower design.

Gilbert, unsure, put his hands on the ground and forced himself to stand. He quickly approached and stopped next to Siby, eager to see what it was.

"What is it? Who gave it to you?"

"Mom," Siby repeated.

"Let me see it, I'll give it back to you right away."

Gilbert, very slowly, raised his arm and held out his hand in a demanding gesture.

"Give it to me, let me see it!"

"No, Mommy gave it to me."

Siby grumbled, hiding her arm behind her back.

Gilbert didn't insist at first. He looked at her for a moment and lowered his head.

Then, looking at her defiantly and crossing his arms, he blurted out:

"If you don't give it to me, I'll take it and throw it in the lake!"

"I'll go tell Mom if you don't leave me alone."

"I'll tell her you ruined my shoes."

Siby looked at her shoes. Gilbert had acted cunningly and finally got what he wanted. He took the piece of metal and immediately walked away as Siby let out a cry of rage. Gilbert lowered his head and shrugged his shoulders to get a better look at the object. He looked at it for a moment and then turned away from Siby, clutching it in his right hand.

"Listen, you don't need this rusty iron. Stop screaming, or I'll go to Mom and tell her what a mess you got here."

Siby became furious, looked at him for a second, then looked up at the sky. Her eyes were shining, as if she were about to cry.

"Give it back, or I'll tell Mom what you did in the forest."

Siby knew she'd lied for the sole purpose of getting him back.

Gilbert turned toward the lake, and as he turned to Siby, telling her to go away, she pushed him into the lake.

"That's what you'll tell Mommy."

The boy tried to swim and stay afloat.

Moving with his arms and legs, he felt the bottom wasn't very deep. The water reached his chest, and, taking a deep breath, he watched Siby walk away.

"Wait, you don't mean to leave me here alone!"

Siby walked a few meters and found herself momentarily near the grass where she had stumbled. She stopped, wondering what had driven her there.

She turned to Gilbert with furious eyes. She looked at the moon, its reflection on the lake; rage gripped her, her only thought being to go and get back what was hers. Gilbert emerged from the water and stormed past Siby, without deigning to look at her. She remained staring at the moonlight and didn't notice her brother returning home without her. She was captivated by that reflection. Her eyes searched for her brother, but she couldn't see him. She heard only footsteps moving as they passed her and walked a few meters away from the lake, approaching the tall grass where she had stumbled.

Siby turned to look for her, and her legs began to run much faster than she could think. Her desire to get her coin back at all costs was such that she threw herself behind Gilbert.

"Leave me alone, can't you see what you've done to me for a coin?!"

He snapped, shaking it off, furious.

"Is it possible that every time I look at you, I have to care more than anything else?"

He turned toward the lake without looking at Siby. And he threw it.

He turned back to his sister.

"There it is!"

Siby turned toward the lake. Without saying anything, her mouth trembling and her chin tucked upward, she burst into tears. In disbelief, she looked at the lake, at her clothes and shoes, thinking about jumping in. She turned to Gilbert, who was walking past the second avenue. She thought again about jumping into the water.

??

Rod and his mother lived outside the village. He was the only child in the house and often helped her. His father never met him. He was very young when he left and never heard from him. Rod knew he was a great man; his mother often shouted at him,

"You'll never be like your father."

He often ran away from home, spending his time searching for stones, making objects, and walking along paths he liked to build, as if expecting someone to visit him one day to show him. His mother forced him to stay outside, often finding streams and throwing pieces of wood into the water to see how far they would reach. He would stare at them and follow the stream's path until he reached its mouth.

One day, following the stream, he climbed into the forest. There he found some strange plants.

Before following the stream that threaded its way through the thick vegetation, he stopped. He wondered what had brought him there. His eyes turned to the sky, instinctively following the flight of the birds that passed overhead. He continued for a few meters, reaching the darkest and thickest part of the forest. He didn't enter it, but simply stared into the darkness.

Rod was attracted to plants and knew how to build objects from pieces of wood. He lowered his gaze for a moment, still wondering what had brought him there. He looked at the forest, spellbound. Something caught his attention. He didn't understand what it was, but the desire to sneak in there drove him from within.

He took a few steps forward. His father used to build strange metal objects, which he didn't use for any specific purpose.

Rod never saw those pieces of metal. He had set out to find something without really knowing what he was looking for. He knew nothing about those objects; his mother had never told him about them.

Over the years, he never learned his true nature. He often argued with his mother. She never told him what had happened to his father. Rod loved to remain silent so he could observe every little sound.

Very often, the knowledge he wanted to have about his father left him perplexed.

Something drove him to search for objects and glimpse the path that always reminded him of himself.

One day his mother noticed he hadn't returned.

Worried, she went into the village to look for Rod.

It was dark, and she left the house, calling out to him.

Something drove her to search. The worry that something might have happened to him pushed her beyond the stream. The moonlight came and went as it receded.

She knew he might be there, still calling out to him. She paused for a moment, the wind lashing the few trees there. Her lips went dry, the wind pushing her in all directions. Her gaze caught something. She realized he wasn't there. Something was watching her. In the darkness, she turned back for a moment to see how far she had gone. She decided to return; she knew Rod didn't usually wander this far, especially at night. She didn't understand where he could be. Something passed over her head. She looked up for a moment to see what it was. As she looked down, she felt something move to her left. For a moment, she was frightened.

She began walking much faster than expected, her head glancing to the left from behind a row of trees. Her apprehension didn't stop her. She'd never encountered such darkness. Rod was on the other side. Her mother paid no attention to what was watching her. When she reached the path leading to the village at a quick pace, she saw something emerge in front of her.

Rod was shaking; he knew he'd gone much further than he should have. His mother grabbed his arm, motioning with her head to move.

They increased their pace; Rod realized something was following them. On the way home, he turned back to see what it was. His mother let go of his arm; they were close to reaching the village gates. The house was a few hundred meters away. Rod touched his arm. The woman didn't know what was bothering Rod; in the darkness, he didn't know what he'd seen or where he'd come from, so scared.

When they got home, she asked him,

"What were you doing in there? You know we're not allowed to walk around at this hour."

She leaned down, her face close to Rod's.

"Dad's not in there."

Rod sobbed, looking away from his mother a couple of times, as if he were afraid, but at the same time he knew he was safe from the danger he had faced in the forest.

"Come on! You don't want everyone to hear me at this hour?!"

Rod didn't utter a word. The light came and went.

After a few weeks, Rod found himself in the upper part of the village. His mother sent him to find some scraps of cloth and buy some seeds. She left him some food in exchange, which he had to give in exchange; a few of those seeds would have been enough.

The old man who was disturbing the seeds was a few meters ahead of the well, in a small house on the right. He lived there and spent whole days sitting near the open door. It was not known why he spent his time sitting and waiting. Rod's mother knew him very well. He was one of the founding fathers of the village. The seeds the ancestors had discovered were entrusted to him. His mother knew the old man didn't talk much.

Rod approached the old man's door, but he didn't notice him.

He couldn't hear very well, so Rod didn't speak to him at first, and the old man continued with his work. Rod took the fruit his mother had given him. He made a move to show them, but the old man seemed unaware of his presence. His movements were very slow. Every now and then he turned to look out the door. While he was selecting the various plants from which he was processing the seeds, he finally noticed Rod. He wasn't surprised. He continued to look at him. He smiled faintly.

Rod handed him the fruit he had, and very slowly the old man dropped the seeds to the ground.

The boy rushed to pick them up. The old man handed him a piece of cloth, which Rod took and wrapped up the seeds he was holding.

Then he silently turned and headed back toward the house. He passed to the right of the well. A large house was under construction.

Gilbert was there. It was much larger than the others. Rod glanced briefly at Gilbert, who was sitting there waiting for his father to finish work. Gilbert's father worked on the construction of the large house in exchange for his service in the forests. Gilbert's father feared the forest. So he made a contribution to the village, helping the few guards who supervised the construction.

Gilbert's father wasn't displeased; no one was forcing his decision to go into the forest.

Gilbert saw Rod pass by him and raised his head. They didn't look at each other out of pure shame.

Rod took a few steps, and Gilbert followed him, turning his head. A man who had been teaching the house stopped in front of Rod, sighed, looked at Gilbert for a moment, and headed toward the well. Rod stopped and looked inside the house for a moment. So he took a few steps back, asking the boy who was sitting on the ground,

"What is it?" He pointed to the house.

Rod didn't talk much. He never did with people he didn't know. In that moment, he was drawn. He had seen a boy like himself and had found the courage.

"My name is Gilbert."

Rod didn't answer, he didn't introduce himself. He stopped in front of Gilbert, who had blond hair and wrinkled clothes. Rod wasn't a man of many words. Without saying anything, he turned around. He took a seed he had kept in the piece of cloth the old man had given him, turned, and took a few steps closer to Gilbert. He held the seed closed in the fist of his right hand. He extended his arm, indicating his hand with his eyes. He opened it in front of Gilbert. Gilbert looked at the hand. Gilbert looked at the hand. He looked at Rod again. Rod showed him with his coconuts what he had in his hand. Gilbert didn't laugh at first. Looking at the hand, he turned to his right for a second. His father came out, calling him.

"Gilbert, Gilbert! Let's go, son!"

Gilbert turned to Rod and took the seed. Rod turned away, filled with shame. So he ran away, passing in front of the house under construction and next to Gilbert's father. The man turned, shocked to see Rod running away at his side. He had no idea who he was. Gilbert and his family had moved to that village a few years earlier. They had come from far away. No one knew their story.

At his father's call, Gilbert rose from the ground and quickly reached the corner of the church where his father was waiting for him.

Gilbert stopped in front of his father. He held out his hand to show him what was inside. Gilbert said nothing, looking at the man with his open hand in front of him. His father looked at what he had in his palm. Without realizing what it was, he took his hand, dropping the seed. He then looked at the seed that had fallen to the ground.

He headed toward the house, leaving the field to his left and the large house behind him. Gilbert turned again to look for Rod.

Meanwhile, the search party prepared to continue their expedition. Steph and Rod remained on guard for most of the night. By dawn, the breeze had extinguished the fire the boys had lit. Smoke still billowed from the ashes, the light morning wind constantly blowing it this way and that. Steph rose from the ground and grabbed her things. The boys weren't fully awake. She saw Rod walking toward the stream.

"Rod, where are you going?"

Rod didn't answer. Steph's voice struggled to break free in the early hours of the morning.

She felt strange pangs. Steph turned back to the tree. She looked inside her bag.

She rummaged through it, searching for the fruit, which she found had retained its color. From when she'd broken it upon finding it. She grabbed it for a moment without removing it from the bag. She followed Rod with her gaze and saw him walk even further away. Some of the boys were showing signs of waking up. Gilbert opened his eyes. Slowly, he moved his arms to pull himself up. Steph passed through the resting boys. She left the fire to her left and walked toward Rod, who was a hundred meters ahead. She couldn't see him.

The commander stopped in front of the boys. He studied them, hesitating for a moment before voicing the command that was springing to mind. He looked at the boy at his feet. "Guys, it's time to go. Wake up!"

Getting no reaction, he repeated the same sentence. The boys began to open their eyes. Some yawned loudly, others moved slowly in those early morning hours.

A boy, his face covered, was already standing a little further ahead. This was unusual behavior.

The commander looked for Steph, but he wasn't where he'd fallen asleep. He turned to look for Rod a little further ahead on the left, where he'd let him rest.

He didn't recognize him at first. The stranger was carrying a bow. It was different from the others he'd seen. It was black. He didn't have a bag or axe, unlike the rest of the men.

Gilbert approached suspiciously, because he remained motionless in front of the group.

"What's wrong? Aren't you preparing like the others?"

The boy kept his gaze on the ground, alert to the situation he was in. He showed no movement at the commander's command; Gilbert continued to approach, suspecting who it was. He turned for a moment to look at the boys waking up. He quickly tried to count them and remember how many there were. As he did, he turned. Again toward the boy with the covered face. He approached, almost bringing them face to face.

"Didn't you hear?"

Gilbert grew suspicious. Without thinking twice, he removed the boy's hood.

He was stunned; his eyes widened. He saw the long hair, the face still covered, and could only glimpse the eyes.

They were a girl's eyes. The commander stared at her for a moment, then turned to Steph as she pushed through the bushes to reach Rod.

He gestured as if calling his name.

He looked the girl in the eyes again.

"Who are you? We don't usually recruit women for these kinds of expeditions."

The girl didn't answer. She lowered her gaze, refraining from speaking. She looked at the commander. Then back at the extinguished fire and the boys.

The girl sensed that the commander was afraid of something. He never usually showed that kind of concern. He looked at her a second time.

"Listen," he said, "There's no place for you here. Don't make me throw you out."

The commander turned his back on her. He walked a few meters away from her. The girl watched him for a moment as he approached the boys. She spoke, not giving a second thought to what she wanted to say.

"The pain in your head you felt last night brought me here!"

Gilbert stopped; frozen in place for a moment, he thought of his sister. He looked into the darkness that reminded him of that night. His eyes changed color. He whirled around, furious. He had touched a sore spot, but he forced himself not to show the anger within him. He knew he had to protect the boys.

He looked at the girl's face. Her eyes were their natural color. No one had seen that look, much less known that her eyes changed at the mere thought.

He waved his hand, wanting to say something, but he didn't bother thinking about what to say.

His right hand pointed to the girl's face. The girl watched his hand move.

Gilbert lowered it again after a moment, letting his arm fall angrily to his side.

Then he walked away. He knew there was no reason to confide his past so openly.

Steph joined Rod at the stream. Rod rinsed his face. Steph paused for a few seconds behind him and glimpsed something beside him. A strange shrub, leafless, dry, and with few branches. Rod turned and noticed his companion staring at the shrub. He remained motionless for a few seconds. Without having to catch his breath.

He asked, "What is that? Haven't you ever seen one?"

Steph didn't answer; she knew it looked similar to others she'd seen before.

He approached the stream and bent down to drink. Rod stood up, unconvinced because Steph hadn't given him an answer. He walked a few meters away and looked at him suspiciously. Lowering his head, he turned, clutching his bag over his right shoulder and his bow over his left. He couldn't explain the reason for so many lapses in his memory.

His mind was tearing him away from reality, making him completely silent and lacking in confidence.

Steph retraced her steps and joined the group. Rod arrived first with some other boys. He saw Gilbert storming away. He felt the tension around the group, but not from the boys. He noticed a presence on his left side. Meanwhile, the girl had covered her face. Rod sensed that something had discouraged Gilbert's attitude. For a moment, he looked around, trying to understand the reason. He knew Gilbert's story, but he had never seen him like this, and he didn't approach to talk to him. That morning, something snapped inside him. As he returned from the stream, something sensed Steph inside him. It was a new sensation he felt. For a moment, he lowered his head with a grimace of pain, as if something had stung his mind. He turned away from the girl, his face covered.

The commander ordered his men to move. They set off again. No one paused. Rod, taking a few steps, began walking in the center of the group. Gilbert turned back without saying anything to the girl and the boys. That morning, strangely, there were no great words. Not even Rod understood what had upset the commander. Steph remained watching the boy, his face covered, who made no move to move. He fell into line behind the group, without looking at the boy. The girl waited a few moments before falling into line as well.

Joseph woke up later than the others that morning. He opened his eyes, looking up at the roof of the house, carefully examining the ceiling. He realized that his half-brothers had been awake for a long time. He didn't hear them in the house, nor Gressy. He rushed out of bed to the table. There he found the strange fruit on his left. He looked back at the table. Meanwhile, Victor was playing outside with his usual stick on the ground; he could hear his words, so he decided to go outside. Victor, at first, didn't notice him because his back was turned. Victor heard the door open.

"There's something on the table."

Joseph approached behind him, watching as he played.

"I've never eaten one."

"Mom left it," Victor said.

He continued playing with his head down.

That morning, Gressy had gone into the village to make some deliveries of embroidered dresses, which had been embroidered a few days earlier. Joseph returned home, something bothering Victor, who was paying no attention to him. The door remained open. His attention lingered on a drawer in a cabinet, but Joseph decided it wasn't the right time to search. Meanwhile, Gressy had reached her house, which was a little further on, on the right side of the square. The old man who lived there had left that space to other people. Gressy made her deliveries. Joseph found himself looking out the window. He could see a path without trees around it. The grass was taller than usual. He looked back, confused by the idea of going there. A moment later, he decided to take that strange fruit and take it with him. He held out his hand. He immediately changed his mind; he wasn't very hungry and it wouldn't help him. Joseph went out and passed Victor, but the latter made no attempt to ask where he was headed.

He rose from the ground, making a gesture toward Joseph.

"Where are you going, Joseph?"

Joseph felt a strange instinct he'd never felt before. He sensed a force so great it was capable of confusing his thoughts.

A strange pull in his chest urged him to take him there. At that moment, Victor asked him where he was going, but he continued without answering. Victor looked at the house and the door that had remained open. He hesitated for a moment, deciding whether to follow Joseph or stay and wait for Vincent's return.

Joseph passed through the tall grass, without looking back. On the left, a low hill rose, and on the horizon, a large expanse of water appeared.

He took a few steps forward, and as he moved further away, he didn't notice that the grass was shorter in some places than expected.

He didn't even look down and didn't notice a cliff. He fell into it, rolling for a few meters. He had never seen a lake before, he didn't even know what it was.

He rolled, rolled again, and again, stopping a few meters from the center.

He stood up, frightened. The grass covered him up to his head. He looked up at the sky for a moment. From there, he could no longer see the village. He looked down at his shoes; his pants had a tear on the right side.

He'd suffered a small cut on his thigh when he fell. The wind stirred the tall grass, which swayed rhythmically. The strange sensation that had brought him there vanished for a moment. He had no idea where he was. For a few seconds, his eyes blurred, unable to see clearly. He rubbed his eyes with his hands. He turned, sensing something moving behind him, and he turned his head this way and that several times to see what it was. Fear gripped him; he wanted to go home. He took a few steps back to the spot where he had fallen. He heard a strange noise coming from his left, like a clicking sound; something like the clattering of two pieces of wood. He saw strange pointed ears jump and move quickly from side to side, unable to distinguish their color from the perceived speed. His instinct was to follow the strange animal with his body, but for a few seconds he remained still. He turned suddenly, walked a few meters back, and began to run away, faster and faster. He climbed the lake bed without looking back.

He ran home. He didn't find Victor outside; the door was wide open. He entered immediately and stopped in front of the door. He checked the bedrooms, first his own, then Gressy's, then the room with the bathtub.

No one was home. The green fruit was still on the table. He went out again. He paused on the threshold, looking for his brothers. He turned and went back inside. The attraction he had felt down in the lake filled him again, he felt a strange tremor in his chest, something causing a friction inside him, like the color of a fire, telling him where to rummage. He remained still for a few minutes and then the fear began to grow. He walked around the house again, checked the bedroom and returned to the kitchen. In the fireplace were several pieces of wood, spaced apart. He returned to the door. The fear passed for a few minutes.

He tried to hear the voices coming from the village. The house's position facing the stream made it impossible to distinguish distant sounds. He looked at the trees in front of him. His eyes widened. Once again, the pull returned. He lowered his gaze, unsure of what was happening. He checked his chest with his hands.

The attraction suddenly vanished.

He looked up in front of him, turned around for a moment inside the house. He checked his bedroom again, then Gressy's. He turned to the cabinet next to the entryway. That attraction flared up inside him again, like a strange signal he'd sensed down by the lake. At first he struggled to trust it. He was thinking of that strange creature who had appeared to him. So he reached out to touch the cabinet there. He heard that signal inside himself. The cabinet had two doors; he opened one, revealing some shelves with silverware, teacups, and a few wooden plates. He didn't notice anything at first. He looked carefully and found a drawer high up on the left. The mere thought that Gressy might return and catch him rummaging through her house shocked him. He turned toward the door to check if anyone was there, then returned his gaze to the drawer. He opened it very slowly, the wood scraping against the cabinet's walls.

There were some wooden cutlery with strange pieces of rusty metal and a bundle of cloth he'd seen before. He touched the cloth with his hand and could feel the object inside. So he took it, quickly closing the drawer and doors. He came out clutching it in his hands. He looked at it for a moment, lowered his head, and felt the same attraction he'd felt when he first found it. He sensed someone approaching.

In an instant, he darted inside and hid near the door so as not to be seen.

He recognized the voices of Vincente and Gressy.

He stuck his head out so as not to be noticed.

Vincente was returning from the fields. He was carrying some fruit he had picked. Gressy noticed that Victor wasn't standing in front of the open door. She quickened her pace and called Joseph.

Joseph emerged from behind the door and hid the object in his pants pocket. He found himself facing Gressy.

"Victor?" She came in, calling him loudly and repeating his name several times.

"Vincent!" she exclaimed.

"Victor isn't here, go look at the stream, go!" she shouted.

Joseph didn't answer and looked out the door, as if to indicate where he was. Gressy came out, saw the disturbed earth on the ground in front of the house, and went back inside.

He turned to Joseph.

"Me," he muttered for more than a second.

Disconsolate, he looked around.

"I saw him outside, he was playing right there, in front of the door.

I walked away for a second. And when I came back, he wasn't there. I went to the lake."

Gressy, after calling out to Joseph, stood up again. Her eyes widened; a few seconds before, they had been filled with anger.

For a moment, something from the past flashed through her mind, and she froze for a moment. Joseph, in that instant, suspected that he might be the reason Victor had disappeared. So he left the house. He sat on the doorstep. With his hands in his hair, he burst into tears.

He watched Gressy sobbing.

He ran to his room. He lay down on the bed with his face in the pillow. His mind was choked with anger, and tears were soaking the pillowcase. Without realizing it, he slipped his right hand under the pillow. His stomach twisted.

He felt a strange sensation. His hand felt warm for a moment. Gressy was out of the house. Pinging, he looked up at the sky. The sunlight blinded him. He began to feel a strange pull coming from outside. He feared something was about to take over.

So she stood up abruptly and turned toward the house. She took a few steps back, frightened by what was building inside her.

She reached the wall with her back to the wall.

She stared into nothingness, the only dirt road in sight. Something startled her, and she touched the side of the door with her hand, as if to orient herself.

Turning only her head, she took a step toward turning her body. She looked inside the house. The sunlight faded intermittently, and a couple of times it suddenly went dark.

Gressy stopped in front of the door. For a few minutes, she held the door with her hand. She slowly entered the house.

She looked to the right, where the table was. She continued a few steps toward Joseph's room. A few strange drops of black liquid were falling from the ceiling.

She looked up to see where they were coming from. She rushed into the boy's room. She sensed something that worried her.

She saw Joseph lying on the bed. Gressy was shaking with fear. She tried to move him to wake him.

"Come on, Joseph! Get up!"

With her hands on his shoulders, she began to shake him. Joseph didn't respond.

Something was crawling on his shoes. He turned sharply, looking down to see what it was. Strange animals were crawling out from under the bed. He shook it again. He knew something was about to happen.

"Joseph, come on, let's go!"

He heard a strange ticking sound coming from outside the door.

Joseph didn't respond. Joseph's breathing was getting louder and louder.

The sun went out intermittently for a second time. So she looked out the bedroom window. She picked Joseph up, lifting him forcefully from the bed and resting his head on her shoulder. She turned to leave. She noticed his hand was all red. Joseph was drenched in sweat. They went outside. A strong wind was rustling the branches of the trees in front of the house. She ran toward the center of the village.

In the forest, the search party was preparing to move on; the sun was almost overhead. Gilbert found another stone. Oddly, a candle was placed on it; it had burned out during the night.

Someone had been there long before them. The commander didn't particularly notice, thinking it might be a candle left during other searches. In the past, candles left on stones meant the expedition had been successful.

"Here's a candle!" Gilbert said, looking at the rest of the group.

A boy said, behind him. Gilbert didn't rush to answer; he stopped in front of the stone. He looked at the candle. Then he turned for a moment, nodding at Rod.

At that moment, Rod understood, looked him in the eyes, and turned to the right, toward the stream.

He suspected something. Steph wasn't feeling well. She was at the back of the group.

Someone laughed at the boy's joke. The boy sensed something, flying toward Steph, who was staring at the ground. He wasn't moving. The commander didn't give any orders; he looked for Rod and saw him staring at the vegetation. He sensed something disturbing him.

That strange sensation of the lake took over his thoughts for a second. He was mesmerized by the view of the village. Then he turned back to the forest and said:

"I know many of you have never been there…"

Steph looked up from the ground. She had heard what the commander had said. Gilbert was about to continue, but he stopped, surprised by Steph's look, and she nodded for the first time. The commander's expression changed, thinking about what he was about to say.

"Let's continue. We have no reason to stop here and waste time."

The group continued their march toward the forest. Rod stood there watching. The girl was at the rear of the group; she had sensed the commander's strange feeling. She looked at Rod. Rod was unaware of the girl; his face was covered. The rest of the group continued on.

So the girl took a few steps toward Rod.

"The commander," she asked.

"Is it always like this?"

The man didn't turn around; his gaze was still fixed on the vegetation. His expression changed when he heard a different voice than usual; he'd never heard one like it since joining the search party. For a moment, he struggled to turn around. He walked away, following the rest of the group. The girl remained, staring at the vegetation, where Rod's gaze was directed. So, at a slow pace, she continued walking, falling in line with the others. Gilbert led the way.

The forest was half a day's walk from where they had stopped for the night. They walked behind the commander; as they approached the top of the hill, the vegetation gradually disappeared. Gilbert began to glimpse the forest emerging halfway behind the hill.

He waved them to a halt. There was no vegetation along that stretch of road. He noticed some bushes sticking out of the ground; they were dry, as if winter had arrived much earlier than expected. He motioned for them to continue. He knew they had to return home with supplies, otherwise the rest of the village would suffer the consequences for quite some time. The boys behind were worried; the two new recruits looked at each other. In a low voice, one asked:

"Ten! Have you noticed the commander? He looks quite unusual.

"They say in the village he lost his sister a long time ago."

The commander heard whispers coming from some of the boys, so he stopped again. He remembered that there should have been another marker at that point, marking the route. His mind clouded over, and he had the strange sensation he'd felt down at the lake.

An old recruit, Tesk, immediately called out to him:

"Commander, commander!"

Steph began to feel strange twinges in her head. She collapsed in pain, touching the side of her head near her right ear.

Suddenly, it got dark; the sun disappeared a couple of times, coming and going intermittently. Gilbert whirled around to check the village behind him. The frightened boys looked up at the sky, their hands ready for the weapons they carried. They looked around cautiously. The commander made no sign of reaction. He looked up at the sky, staring at the sun.

Rod was at the end of the group. He glanced back and turned sharply toward the forest, searching for something that had previously haunted the other search party. Birds in the trees took flight. For a few minutes, he feared the worst. He suspected the girl behind him, so he turned again. The sun disappeared intermittently a couple of times. The wind began to stir the trees. Rod sprinted toward the stream on the right, and Gilbert noticed his movement but remained still, gazing at the village.

The boys, gripped by panic, looked at the motionless commander.

"Commander! What's happening?"

The group noticed that the birds had taken flight, flying in all directions and making strange noises.

Frightened by something, they passed overhead, heading toward the village.

Rod, walking toward the stream, could notice the various shrubs.

Gilbert didn't respond to the boys at first. Everyone was expecting orders from him. The commander stared straight ahead, while memories of his sister Siby took over. With a frozen gaze, he turned toward the forest, his eyes narrowed in defiance.

Steph couldn't move because of the pain he was feeling.

A strange sensation prevented him from raising his head and looking around.

Rod reached the stream. Raising his head, he watched the flocks of birds heading toward the village. Taking a few steps forward, he remembered there were no trees there. The stream ceased. He could hear the flocks of birds in the distance. The cold forest air hit his face. He looked at the mountain.

He thought, "Why now?"

Every slight movement of the trees, every perceptible detail, captured his attention. His arms, stretched out at his sides, stiffened.

He continued following the stream's path, though. He didn't know where it would lead him. He would conduct his search alone. He set off without looking back or warning Gilbert.

or warn Gilbert.

The commander remained motionless, and the rest of the group trembled with fear, wondering repeatedly why he wasn't responding to their questions.

Ten, the veteran recruit, had joined the search party a few years after Gilbert. He had come from overseas. They didn't know his story or how he had arrived there. No one ever heard of his parents; some doubted that even Ten knew why he had come from so far away. He was cared for by a man in the village, only slightly older than Gilbert's father.

Ten was a few years older than Gilbert.

He arrived in the village accompanied by a man; he was only twelve years old at the time. He immediately noticed that the village was sparsely populated. The frustration of leaving his hometown saddened him. He constantly researched the area and often traveled south, where he had come from. Several years later, Ten was convinced to join the research corps.

Gilbert had taken over as commander at just sixteen; at the time, there was no fear that the terror might return. The boys joined the search parties to help feed the village by discovering plants and fruits that could be used as ingredients in teas that alleviated the pain often caused by the weather changes.

Gilbert initially resisted him; his story raised doubts and perplexities, and the villagers did not trust him.

Ten didn't mind at first; he was aware of being a stranger. He had no relationship with the group, or with anyone, really: he didn't lend himself to socializing with other people. His mind was always on the other side of the ocean, a vast expanse of water from which he often remembered his origins. He tried to remember why he had left his homeland. Very often, he left alone. In the village, Tne was seen as a misfit. Those who tried to spend time with him didn't understand his behavior; most of the time, he was silent and showed obvious signs of nervousness when speaking to people.

At the age of seventeen, he left to explore the coast; he went further than he could have imagined, without telling the man of the house who cared for him. For weeks, no one heard from him.

Ten had brought some food with him, but after a couple of days it ran out, but that didn't matter much to him. On the beach, he found fish unknown to the village. He walked east across the cliffs. Instinct guided him.

One day, in the midst of a storm, a swollen river blocked his path. So he headed toward the river's source, climbing north into the forest. About a hundred meters from the river, he found a small shelter, a half-ruined wooden house. He wasn't sure what had brought him there.

The few supplies he had brought helped him get through the night. He was soaking wet, the water seeping into the rotten wood from every angle. At that moment, he decided it would be best to return. The storm was keeping him awake; he couldn't sleep. He wanted to get out and return to the beach. He rose from the ground and headed toward the shore, following a strange light that called to him, shining through the trees in front of him. It seemed to him that something was moving behind him. He thought it was someone and turned sharply. The swollen river drowned out all other sounds, but he could hear footsteps behind him. Something was wrong. They were so unusual human footsteps. He quickened his pace without looking back. When he reached the beach, a strange animal in the water reflected the light it carried within it. He turned to look back; the river was a few hundred meters from the expanse of water. He turned to look back sharply. The strange animal didn't follow him to the beach. He felt a strange fear, the loneliness of finding himself alone returning to him. He had never felt like he was being followed by something that put him in such danger.

On his way back to the village, Ten found strange objects. A skull with a strange long snout and a strange bone protruding from its head. at nose height. He had never seen anything like it. Pieces of wood were scattered everywhere, and one in the shape of an eye caught his eye. A strange piece of wood with an extremely strange outline. He had never seen anything like it; it showed the grain of a non-human body.

He knew there were no people or things like that overseas. Something in that storm had awakened a strength, and his soul was satisfied in rediscovering those strange beings no one else knew about. No one but him knew what the sea had shown him.

He walked to find his way home. In the village, the people and the search party wondered where he had gone.

Ten had been missing for a few weeks. When he returned, the villagers became suspicious of him. Gilbert believed he was hiding something. He was the only one to ask where he had gone.

"Where have you been, Ten? The village was worried…"

Ten didn't reply, as usual. The commander's attention was something he wasn't used to.

"Trying to figure out who you are?"

Ten looked him in the eye, his gaze unconcerned.

He knew he shouldn't tell anyone about the object he'd found and what he'd seen down there.

"South, near the sea," he replied.

"South, near the sea," he replied.

Gilbert was suspicious for a couple of seconds; his demeanor was calm, but he sensed something was unsaid. He couldn't explain that need to cross borders, and what had driven him so far away from everyone. That yearning for his origins and where he came from intrigued him.

Ten, he approached Gilbert.

"Commander!" he exclaimed, shaking.

"What are we going to do? We can't stay like this…"

Gilbert didn't speak; Ten could see the pain on his face. The other boys looked around worriedly. The commander remained silent until he made a decision. His was an instinctive choice. They were in danger.

"T-T-Ten. There's a shelter there. In the forest at the foot of the mountain. You'll find a small shelter."

Ten nodded.

"Aren't you coming with us, Commander? I've never failed myself on that route."

Gilbert stood still for a few seconds, unable to find any other words that could help the rest of the group. The girl and Rod had disappeared.

He turned very slowly, looking at the mountain.

"I know it, Ten. I know it," he said, his gaze fixed on him. The rest of the group couldn't hear what they were discussing.

"I met her a long time ago, something brought her with it. I lost sight of her for a second. One second she was there, the next, she wasn't. I realized I had to entrust the command to others, because of my fear."

"This isn't the time, Commander. How far is the shelter from here?"

"Years spent trying to understand my fears and prevent them from taking over. Courage alone. If I'd only had…"

"Commander! The group is panicking. We have to go!"

"Three hours. By the time we get there, we'll already be in danger. The forest is his home."

Ten realized something was preventing Gilbert from taking control. His gaze remained fixed once again on the fact that he was carrying within him, which could put everyone at risk, ruining the hero's quest.

Gilbert tried to react. He had two options: return home, suffering once again over the disappearance of innocent people, or search the forest for answers and return with more concrete evidence to put the village out of danger.

Ten joined the rest of the group and asked if anyone knew about the shelter.

The commander exclaimed,

"Let's go! I'll show you."

Everyone looked at each other strangely, doubting whether it was a good idea to go all that far.

"Commander, what about the village? They must know…" said one of the new recruits.

Gilbert, turning toward the mountain, whispered:

"They already know."

In the village, Gressy began to raise the alarm. She reached the center of the market, holding the still-sleepless Joseph in her arms, screaming and calling for help.

"My son Victor!"

"Come back to your homes, everything will be fine."

A man in his sixties, near the fountain, began shouting repeatedly,

"He's coming back, he's coming back!"

Alarming the villagers. None of them knew the real danger they were facing.

One of the guards suddenly approached the old man, silencing him. He escorted him home.

The few who remembered what had happened in the past were asked not to tell anyone, or else they would have to leave the village for their own safety.

The guards had no idea what awaited them. The sun was not a major cause for concern for them. They tried to restore order and calm those present.

"Go home, protect yourselves with what you have. Lock the doors tightly. And don't leave until you receive further orders."

Gressy initially didn't listen to what they were saying to the people. She approached the guards, worried about her son Victor, begging for help.

"Victor, my son, he's missing."

"Go home, Gressy."

"Please, I don't know what to do. Has he put himself in danger?!" Turning to the villagers, he asked again.

"Has anyone seen my son Victor?"

Her concern frightened the people at the assembly point.

"And Vincent? Doesn't anyone know anything?"

The guards sent her away, and one of them decided to walk her home.

"Look, ma'am, this worry will put everyone at risk."

Gressy didn't hesitate to answer immediately, as the guards didn't know the village's history as well as she did. She knew something had put her son in danger. She couldn't say much more about what had happened, as the stories of the past were now forgotten. Fear was seen as something to be avoided, it was viewed by the guards as suspicious.

As they walked toward the house, the guard watched Gressy carefully, trying to understand her intentions. Her primary concern at that moment was ensuring the well-being of the village, but he understood that Gressy was in danger, and looking into her eyes, he realized there was much more the guards needed to know.

Something that had shocked her. Gressy, unable to speak for fear, resisted.

"I can't go home. For my son's sake, I have to find it!".

Joseph was still in her arms, his hand even redder than expected. The guard insisted, and they continued toward the house. Gressy turned to watch the other people, obedient to the orders, begin returning to their homes, listening to advice on supplies and how to stay safe.

Gressy muttered under her breath, thinking about how to organize a solo search for her son. Time was passing, and Victor might be even further away than expected. A few steps from the house, the guard saw something moving behind the stream.

"Wait," he said, turning to Gressy.

"Who's there?" He took the gun in his hand, slipping it from the belt at his back, and slowly approached. For a moment, the stream stopped moving. The water dried up. The guard momentarily lost concentration, staring at the stream. Something was coming closer and faster. Gressy could hear its footsteps, while the gunman kept his gaze fixed on the stream, stunned by fear. The footsteps were getting closer and closer, faster and faster.

"Stay back, stay back," the guard urged to protect the woman, who was still carrying Joseph in her arms.

He returned his gaze to those steps. Suddenly, he stopped to observe some trees; bushes covered their trunks, beyond the stream.

He could hear rapid breathing and took a few more steps, approaching even closer, very cautiously. He crossed the stream, drawing the weapon he had in his hand. His breathing, as he approached, became more and more labored.

"Victor, is that you?" the guard asked.

He approached the bushes, carefully making his way through them.

He saw a head appear a little lower to the left. He heard a worried breath.

"Vincent!" he exclaimed.

"Where have you been?"

"Vincent," said Gressy.

Her eyes spoke louder than her voice, her face didn't move, they watched her son emerge from behind the bushes. The guard approached, lowering himself to his knees.

"Where have you been?"

Vincent didn't answer out of fear. His breathing was labored. The guard could hear his heartbeat. Rising to his feet, the man put his arm around Vincent's neck and escorted him away.

Vincent looked behind him, turned back to the guard, and for a moment calmed down. He didn't say a word. He saw Gressy on the other side of the stream, with Joseph in her arms.

"Mom!"

He shouted, running toward her and hugging her.

"Where have you been? Did you find Victor?"

She asked, still shaken by the shock. In that moment, she sensed something had changed in Vincent. She tried to search his thoughts, scanning his face as he looked at the guard. She darkened; something had gripped her family. She considered the events of the past.

"No," she said, looking at the stream on the right.

"I thought I heard it there.

Joseph? What's wrong with Joseph? Why isn't he awake?

Gressy didn't answer. The guard made his way behind the bushes, investigating what might have scared Vincent. Five minutes later, he returned.

Gressy didn't move. Her shocked expression hadn't changed. She thought briefly of Steph, who was with the search party. She was worried about Victor; she had a strange feeling. She began to tremble.

"Gressy! You can't stay here," warned the guard. "Go inside and don't tell anyone what happened to you. I'll send someone as soon as I get back with the other guards."

The woman's thoughts increasingly clouded her ability to respond.

The guard realized something inside Gressy had taken over; she couldn't fight back against that intense feeling that had made her more self-possessed.

"Gressy, Gressy! Go back inside."

Gressy looked at the guard.

"Victor." Her voice was exhausted.

The man understood and without another word escorted them home.

The guard ran back to the fountain square, where some guards were stationed. He saw no other people.

He approached them and asked, "Where are all the others?"

His companions turned around, and one of them asked where he'd been all this time.

"Gressy, we found Vincent. Where are the villagers?"

"In their homes. Better to avoid any further mishaps for now."

"Captain, is there something wrong?!"

"There's no captain, we've never experienced such concern.

We've maintained this calm for years, but now the past is revolting before we've even known what we have to face."

"Gressy, there's something strange about her. She might know much more than we do."

"The past hasn't helped us..."

"The son is missing. He could be of help to keep everyone safe. We should talk again."

The others remained still, no one saying a word for a minute. One of them noticed the apprehension on his face.

"You two will keep watch throughout the village until sunset. The two of us will go to Gressy," he ordered.

Some of the guards were once part of the search party. Back then, they were recruited for the sole purpose of bringing supplies to the village.

None of them truly knew the danger or the history of the past. Occasionally, some story was told by the groups as they walked through the forest.

Soc was the guard who paid extra attention to the group when Gilbert wasn't there; there was no captain or commander at the time. No one knew how Gilbert had gained that post, but everyone had heard of the danger he and his sister had put themselves in. Some of them despised him for his role, others thought the experience had given him a certain authority. What the village had faced long ago was one of Gilbert's first disconcerting episodes.

Soc was in the village with the villagers, awaiting the arrival of his companion Riz before making any decisions. People were asked to return to their homes. As the sun set, people locked themselves in their homes, locking them in the hope that the danger would not return. They were unprepared, imagining that this nightmare would only last a few days. They were asked, in keeping with ancient tradition, to light oil lamps made from wild herbs. They produced a green flame that could stay lit even during the day, invisible in the sunlight. These lamps were once used to drive away any danger, keeping out of reach any approaching illness.

Soc was born in that village and was slightly younger than Gilbert. They never met, despite his father being part of the search party. Once, when the bodies were forced to be separated in the forest, his father had been among those who never returned to the village. Soc was only thirteen when he learned of his father's disappearance.

His father had taken over in those final years. Soc was never able to learn the truth; some told him he'd simply gotten lost in the forest, and each time he sensed they were hiding something from him. They were afraid they'd scare him, and few, if any, knew what the search forces had faced on those expeditions. The loss of his father was the greatest pain he faced in his young age.

He ran away from home, even though his mother tried to stop him, and disappeared for a couple of days. He walked along the stream until he reached the forest, then headed west.

He walked for quite some time, not looking back. His intention was to find evidence about his father or the search party that hadn't returned a few days earlier.

He entered the thick vegetation, found the usual candles, and without realizing it, overstepped his bounds.

He continued for hours and hours. Finally, tired and confused, he stopped and looked around. He shouted his father's name several times and continued searching, fearful that he wouldn't be able to find him. Frightened, he carefully studied the vegetation around him and noticed a thicket rising on a hill to his right. Looking for some sign of the search party's passage, he moved behind their trunks. He found ash. Smoke rose from it every now and then. The wind from the forest blew against his face, and his concentration lingered for a moment as he watched the trees on the hill move. For a moment, he had the feeling that it was getting dark and that black clouds were appearing behind him, blocking out the daylight. He turned sharply, but realized it had only been an illusion. He turned to go back, but he couldn't find the road. He walked far enough. The sun had almost set. He accelerated to find the stream he'd wandered away from. He noticed something had changed compared to a few hours earlier. He headed south to follow the stream that led toward the village. He found even more vegetation, even more trees. Confused, he tried to go back, toward those smoke signals.

He continued walking, immersing himself in the vegetation. The trees and plants grew much taller than him as he advanced. The sun had almost set, and the few remaining minutes of light frightened him even more. Out of fear, he began to run.

He felt like he was getting closer to the smoke signal, but he remained at the same distance. The vegetation prevented him from moving quickly. Daylight had given way to darkness when he found himself at the edge of a precipice. Another forest stretched out before him. He looked down to assess its height. The landscape around him no longer seemed the same. He realized he wasn't in the same place as when he'd crossed the forest line.

He was in an unfamiliar place. The chasm confused him, and he looked around for a way out. The smoke signals he had followed faded into the night, disappearing from his sight. He turned quickly to find a place to take shelter; he knew he couldn't go back and that the night in the forest was dangerous. The insistent return of his father confused him. Panicking, he returned to the precipice again. He had to find something to eat. He realized how foolish he had been to go further than anyone else would ever go. His had been an angry gesture. He sat down near a tree. Night was increasingly dominating the sky. He spent a couple of hours sitting, looking over the chasm and wondering if any of the search party had survived, hoping they would come find him. His eyes followed the forest illuminated by the moonlight. Something moved among the vegetation. He stood up, the instinct to lean further out to see over the cliff tormenting him. He looked down, watching the trees move. He turned to look behind him, feeling the sensation of something watching him. He glimpsed an arm moving quickly behind the trees, recognizing only the color blending with the branches. His eyes widened with fear. For a moment, he thought the moonlight might have confused him. He froze as something began to move more and more. He noticed a tree about to fall, so he moved, following the precipice. He sprinted for about ten meters, turning back to see what had happened. The tree was no longer there. Out of fear, he continued to run, surrounded only by the silence of the forest and his own breathing. He entered the forest, trying to make his way toward the stream, but he couldn't figure out where it was going. Fear gripped him and pushed him deeper into the forest. He walked away for more than twenty minutes and realized he was in another part of the forest when the vegetation around him disappeared. The trees were spaced apart, lined up as if someone had planted them there. He lowered himself with his hands on his knees. His shortness of breath clouded his head, and he could feel the pounding in his temples. He felt something moving behind him. He began to run again, plunging into the even darker forest. Only the moonlight was there to guide him. Something was moving more and more. He could hear footsteps following him. Like his own. It was as if three people were running behind him. He began to run again. His footsteps were getting closer and closer; he could see bushes near some rocks to his left. As he got closer and closer, he stumbled. For a moment, he looked back from the ground, unable to move his foot, stuck in the roots protruding from the ground. He freed himself. He started running again, and something flew in front of him, passing to his left, from the direction of the bushes. He could only glimpse the upper part of its body with three heads, hairless, not like the usual birds you saw around. It had an object on one of its heads, which reflected in the light. Soc moved in the opposite direction, towards the mountain. Meanwhile, the footsteps became more and more insistent, ever closer, the strange animal moving faster and faster. Soc turned towards the part of the forest that was illuminated by the moon. The point where he had entered completely. He had never seen anything like it move at that speed. He began walking slowly, moving backward. He stared at the patch of light in front of him.

It was about ten meters away, moving step by step, trying not to make a sound. He lowered his disappointed breathing, straining to remain silent. The footsteps were getting closer and closer.

When it reached his line of sight, it remained still. He could hear the crunching of leaves and the thumping of feet on the ground. It was a strange animal with five legs and no head. The moonlight blurred its color. Soc's eyes widened, unable to breathe. The animal took a few steps in his direction, but a strange sound caught his attention from the other side of the forest, and it began to move in the opposite direction. Soc continued to stare at it, stunned as it moved away, fear leaving him there, thinking that his father could have disappeared because of such a beast and that the rest of the group couldn't handle such a large animal.

"Corsair," Soc said softly.

Avoiding the illuminated area, he preferred to continue in the shadows, hoping to quickly find his way home. He continued for a good half hour, unable to find any sign of the path home or the stream he remembered crossing. He could see that the forest was divided into two parts: on the shaded side was the thickest vegetation where the moonlight couldn't penetrate; on the other side, the forest with the trees spaced apart. The moon appeared and disappeared behind the clouds. The fog descended from the mountain. It was like a wall blocking his path, or perhaps it was there to protect him from whatever threatened him at that moment. He lowered his gaze to the ground, unsure of what he was getting himself into. For a second time, his heart palpitations returned, and he felt the cold touch his face. He couldn't see more than a meter away. He looked up for a moment. The forest grew thicker, its fog obscuring his view. Moving through branches and bushes that scratched his arms and face, he closed his eyes for a moment. Finally, he found himself immersed in a different kind of vegetation and turned back to see what he had left behind. The fog remained there, blocking his view of the trees and the stretch of woods he had passed through. He turned forward again, taking a few steps. He heard the sound of the stream and found it not far away. Behind him, the fog had disappeared, giving way to the reality he had left behind.

Meanwhile, the search party was making its way toward the shelter. The commander knew they had to find evidence, and that an old Malay man was leading the way, recalling the village's past trauma. It most likely had something to do with the situation Gilbert himself had experienced as a child. Something had changed in his appearance, but he sensed a new threat, one that was bringing with it an unknown side. Gilbert continued his march at the head of the group. The boys trembled with every step, unprepared for the issues they would face, and feared the worst. Something terrifying awaited them in the forest. Gilbert knew they had to find out what was taking over; for many years now, search parties had no longer been prepared for situations like this. Even Steph had forgotten what the group needed to face that danger; he couldn't bear another burden, his problems with his past kept him from always being clear-headed. Gilbert realized he was the only one who had to make decisions. As they reached the edge of the forest, he looked at the group. Exhausted, he said:

"Rod! We're almost there!"

Hearing no response, he turned to the group. None of the boys spoke.

"Where's Rod?" he asked.

The boys looked at each other, making sure everything was okay. One of the recruits began to move and fidget with a look of great concern.

The boys feared something from Gilbert's face.

"Who's Rod?! Commander!"

Gilbert feared he was in grave danger. His expression said it all about Rod. He couldn't say anything else before the new recruit turned and added:

"It's my first few days, and I've found myself in this situation."

Gilbert understood the gravity of the situation when, looking at the group, he noticed that the girl was no longer there.

Everything began to swirl in his mind. Rod wasn't used to this kind of thing; he wouldn't abandon the group like that. The commander tried to calm the group; he knew he had to look after them more than anything else.

Steph didn't understand; his mind was drifting in a direction that was taking him further and further away, but suddenly he realized Gilbert's concern. Gilbert looked at him for a moment and lowered his head in pain. The tension in the group was rising; Steph was the only one who could somehow know the solution to the danger and contribute to the group if there was any support.

The rest of the group was growing more and more agitated. Gilbert understood that the new recruits couldn't and shouldn't know what awaited them in the forest. They had to reach the shelter before sunset. They needed a place that would give them safety. Turning back could be quite dangerous; it could mean letting something unleash itself in the forest without knowing the full extent of the danger.

Gilbert was unprepared; what shocked the group at that moment didn't help him, so it was simply an expedition. They found themselves in the midst of a catastrophe that was about to resurface after decades, carrying with it that mysterious object that only he knew.

The memory of his sister and the sensation of hearing her voice transported him to another world. He turned toward the mountain, saying to the boys.

"Come on, we're almost there, we have to get to the shelter. We can't afford to stay here and lose our minds right now."

One of the new recruits, turning to the rest of the group, exclaimed: "Are you kidding?! Isn't this a game?

We want to know, Commander. Your pride won't be enough to keep us alive."

Gilbert approached him and tried to calm him down, speaking softly.

"Listen, now is not the time to talk. We have to get there."

The new recruit looked at the commander. He had never spoken like that before. His expression was quite unusual.

"Commander, what about the sun?"

"Commander, how long?"

The group was starting to ask too many questions, but Gilbert couldn't risk losing control.

"Listen. We didn't come here to understand. Our march must continue, our mission begins now, it's crucial for the rest of the village. What awaits us now is a mystery."

He reflected, looking toward the mountain.

"We must continue!" he shouted.

The boys looked at each other in astonishment. The commander never alerted the group, leaving them in a state of uncertainty.

Gilbert opened his bag, grabbing the object he was carrying; it would give him the courage to fully assume his responsibilities.

Steph turned back for a moment toward the village, his mind still clouded. He was the only one, along with Gilbert and Rod, who knew the edges of the forest and the placement of the candles placed in previous years. The sunlight was fading as they approached the shelter. Gilbert ordered his men to move faster; he knew it was a safe place left by the old search parties.

They had initially built it to carry supplies they couldn't carry, but it was later used as a shelter for the few survivors who, many years before, had to face what lurked in the darkness. Night forced them to take refuge there. The walls protected them from what lay beyond.

"Come on, move!" Gilbert said.

Steph understood why they were headed there when a wave of thoughts, fluctuating within him, opened up, and he felt calm for a few minutes. But then the sharp pains returned, and the pain became suffocating.

"We're almost there. We'll spend the night here," the commander announced, pointing to the shelter a few hundred meters away.

"Start gathering some wood, and we'll build a fire outside the shelter."

Step by step, they entered the forest. Ten realized that the shelter was in a location he had passed many times before without ever realizing it existed. It was as if something had made it appear in that instant to protect the group and buy them time. Some began gathering wood, others stayed with Ten and Gilbert. As they continued their march, the shelter gradually decreased in size. From the mountain side, as someone noticed, it seemed much larger than it had when they were close to it. Rod and the girl had completely disappeared, but the commander didn't order the group to search. Only Ten had noticed their absence and thought it was time to take action.

Impatiently, upon arriving at the shelter, he asked Gilbert,

"Commander, is anyone missing?"

Gilbert guessed what he was referring to.

"I know, but I can't put the group at risk. There's nothing to worry about. We'll be safe here."

Ten replied thoughtfully,

"What awaits us here after what happened a few hours ago? They have a right to know."

Gilbert turned, trying to project the confidence of a commander.

"Listen, Ten, the reason we're here is so we don't endanger the village. The only thing left to do is find out what's happening so we can protect them and not alarm the group."

Part of the group was preparing to approach the shelter, while the others were busy gathering some wood. Ten recognized that part of the forest. He had lived there as a child, in that experience. No one knew as well as he did the truth it held and the danger he had faced as a boy. The fear of encountering his past again worried him.

"Command!" Ten said,

"The past is a nasty beast. If there's anything I can do, I'm at your disposal."

Gilbert froze as he tried to open the shelter door.

"Start looking around for candles; we'll need them. Although I don't think their location has changed."

Ten nodded. He began searching around the shelter. The sky was turning blue overhead, while the night light appeared in the distance. Some of the boys began carrying pieces of wood to the entrance. Some others were grabbing oil to prepare for the fire. Others dispersed a few steps away, gathering more supplies.

Gilbert asked one of the boys for help.

A young man with blond hair approached him.

"Yes, Commander!"

"Come on, we have to lift this piece of wood."

They unlocked the old wooden lock and managed to open the door. The upper part of it crumbled. They took a few steps back to avoid being hit, frightened.

"This old shack almost ran over us."

Gilbert, at first, didn't look at the boy; his head was down, staring at the pieces of wood on the door. Then he looked at his face: his expression was quite calm, showing no signs of fear or contempt at being there at that moment, unlike the others, who show signs of tension and nervousness. His hair was shining, and his calmness made something he was carrying in his bag vibrate.

Steph approached Gilbert.

"Commander!"

Steph looked at the commander, struck by Gilbert's gaze, which, while staring, made no response. Something was absorbing his attention. Steph called him a second time.

"Commander. The boys haven't lit the fire yet. Some of the boys haven't returned."

Gilbert didn't turn around, absorbed in the fact that the boy had shown him the nature of his calm. Steph called him again.

"Commander, there's something. Some haven't returned yet."

Gilbert felt something move in his bag and instinctively reached in without showing concern. He grabbed the object in his bag, squeezing it without removing it.

The vibration that only he could feel stopped emanating. For a moment, he relaxed, all his tension suddenly gone.

As if nothing had happened, he exclaimed.

"Steph, take care of the fire."

Glance at the boy and added,

"I've never felt such a presence in the group before."

Steph, turning again to Gilbert,

"Commander, my head. Those things are back. Something's wrong."

Ten, meanwhile, had moved away from the shelter and hadn't yet found any candles. He continued for about ten meters, descending, with the shelter disappearing behind him into the darkness of the forest.

He began to find a few stones without candles on them. Then another, and then another.

Step began to feel strange sensations. Something in his bag was drawing his attention. Then again in his arms, he sensed something getting closer and closer to their position. He could hear its movement in the forest. The rest of the group continued gathering, and he made a move to light the fire. He began arranging the wood, starting with the smaller branches. He noticed that one of the group had brought oil with him. He couldn't wait; he sensed danger near the shelter; something was threatening their position. He couldn't afford to wait, risking putting the group at risk by revealing his feelings. He grabbed a bag of arrowheads he had with him, tapped it on a rock, and smoke began to rise.

As his mind began to show him strange places in the forest, his heart beat faster with every step. Three found the remains of some candles; something had been there long before they reached the shelter. Strangely, Ten wondered why the shelter was still intact. The night light was fading among the passing clouds, enveloping the forest in darkness. Something moved behind Ten. Steph began to sweat.

When the commander was inside the shelter, he called the entire group's attention and came out, shouting,

"Guys, it's time to go back."

Watching Steph trying to light the fire, he asked,

"Where are the others?"

Steph didn't answer, continuing to light the fire, tormented by something that frightened him. After a few minutes, Steph looked up, drawn by the commander's attention. His mind continued to race.

"Commander, there's something coming our way."

Gilbert looked at Steph. He knew he was accustomed to such symptoms due to the ailments the mind caused him. He looked around for a moment; some of the boys were returning to the shelter. As he watched them, he asked,

"Where do I give the others?"

"Where are the others?"

A recruit replied, "Commander, the darkness of the forest prevented me from seeing the others' positions."

Gilbert looked back into the forest. The fading moonlight, the only fire illuminating the position in front of the shelter, illuminated the position. Gilbert turned to the blond-haired boy. Pointing at him, he called out.

"Boy! What's your name?"

The recruit turned and answered Gilbert.

"Sid, Commander."

"Run. Sid!" she ordered, raising her voice.

Something moved behind her, causing a rustling in the trees and drawing everyone's attention. They heard the sound of branches snapping, the thud of a tree falling, and the sound of bones cracking in the distance. With the fire burning, they didn't notice the flame change color; their attention was focused on the forest.

Sid rushed to find Ten, running and calling his name. He advanced about ten meters, the darkness of the forest obscuring his vision and the silence enveloping him. He went a couple more meters before tripping on a stone and rolling down. He stopped at the foot of a tree, dazed by pain. He struggled to get up from the ground. Someone from behind the tree covered his mouth, signaling him to be quiet. Behind them, a creature caught his attention, taking small steps to move around them. Ten recognized it; it looked like the same one he had glimpsed as a boy. They rose very slowly from the ground, making small movements. When Sid glimpsed part of the figure, his agitation stopped every single movement. The pirate was about ten meters away. Sid began to sweat, terror preventing him from moving his arms and legs, and he began to utter incomprehensible words in a low voice. Ten turned to look at him and realized it wasn't just fear clouding his mind; he was in a trance. She tapped him on the shoulder. Sid woke up, with a tree trunk behind him.

Ten turned his head very slowly behind him. The corsair had sensed their presence. The branches on the ground crumbled along with the leaves. Sid's eyes widened as his companion held a hand over his mouth to prevent him from breathing. The two remained still in front of the tree as the creature approached from behind them. It was two meters tall, headless, and moved only on its legs. Sid counted five, while he continued to sweat profusely, holding back his agitation. His hands became wet. The creature could only hear its breathing; at that moment, there were no other sounds to distract it as it drew ever closer.

In front of the shelter, all attention was on the forest and the sounds coming from it. Steph was bent on his knees, listening. The new recruit turned to the commander, whispering,

"Are those the others? Commander!"

Gilbert didn't answer, his gaze completely absorbed.

Steph began to feel strange twinges again, and she bent over in pain, this time even more severe. She collapsed to the ground near the fire, as screams rose from the forest. Some of the boys started to move toward the vegetation to lend help, but an old recruit, Tesk, stopped them.

Ten and Sid noticed the creature's movements change as it heard those screams. On the ground behind the creature, beneath the leaves, a strange object lit up. It emitted a bright light. For a few moments, the creature stopped moving toward them, then moved away as if frightened by the aura it emanated. The blue light, intermittently, emitted signals that frightened the creatures around the shelter. Ten approached. Sid followed and stood still, staring at the light, while his companion dropped to his knees. Ten picked up an object from among the leaves; a strange stone lit up, sending out beams of light with a starlike glow. Frightened by the strange object and not knowing what it was, Sid approached and asked,

"What is it?"

The other didn't answer at first, knowing there was something important to discover. Something capable of scaring away the beasts he'd faced in the past. The frightened search party turned their gaze toward that strange light as the commander ordered his men not to stray and assigned Steph to check the perimeter. Ten immediately put the spearhead back in his bag and turned, signaling his companion to return to the shelter. Gilbert had meanwhile reached them, following the beams of light, and asked them what had happened. Ten opened the bag, revealing the object.

"Did this drive those beasts away? Should we show it to Steph?"

Gilbert looked it over quickly; it looked like one of the spearheads Steph built.

"Was the light coming from here? Don't show it to anyone; I'll take a look at it myself."

Grabbing his arm, she stopped him, looking him in the eye.

"Did you hear that?"

Ten replied and, huffing, set off toward the shelter. Gilbert scanned the area where they'd found the stone, wondering why such a thing had been left there. He had a strong feeling that someone was helping them; the spearhead-shaped stone had certainly chased away those monsters. He hadn't been able to see the creature, but he could only hear the screams of his captured companions. There were other monsters out there; it was hard to imagine how many there were. Sid stood there, watching the commander as he continued to search the area.

"Commander? What are you looking for?"

Gilbert continued with his head down, trying to figure out what had brought the stone to that spot, but he found no trace. He stopped when he noticed Sid waiting for him in silence.

"Come on, let's go back."

Sid stared at a point in the darkness, only the moonlight illuminating part of the forest. He looked at her as if he'd experienced something similar before, then turned and started walking after Gilbert.

Ten had already reached the base. Steph was still standing, staring at the fire when I passed him. Tan entered the shelter without looking at anyone or asking his companions anything.

Gilbert and Sid also reached the shelter, and the commander immediately asked,

"Have you found the others?"

"Nothing yet, Commander," replied a recruit. "Find the others and tell them to go back.

We'll spend the night here, we'll rescue whoever remains on guard."

The commander entered the shelter. Steph fed the fire before returning, some of the boys followed him, emerging from behind the forest. Once inside the shelter, they sat down on the ground; there were no chairs or tables in the storeroom; it was completely empty. It was late at night, and the cold mountain air was making itself felt. Some of them were starting to find space inside, others were still lingering outside the shelter. Gilbert began assigning guard shifts for the night, asking his men to be extremely attentive. He warned Steph to prepare with what he had. Whatever happened, they were not to leave the shelter. At the slightest sound of danger, they were to alert the commander. Everyone present settled in, finding a place in the shelter to spend the night. They didn't know what awaited them. Steph thought the fire might help. Ten rummaged in his bag and passed the spearhead through his hands. He avoided He knew what it might mean. He looked at his companion for a moment. He was sitting near the entrance door on the left, while Gilbert was at the back on the right. None of them said a word; they knew they'd lost men, and the fear that something might be out there kept them from breathing. The last of the boys returned, their faces grim.

"No one has been found, Commander."

Gilbert lowered his head.

"Prepare something to spend the night with, the supplies you gathered. Make sure they last you for these few days."

They were long days for Gilbert, his imagination leading him to experience what he lost so long ago. The idea that it could have repercussions on the fate of the group silenced him; he was not one for many words.

He sighed, easing the pressure, while the thought of his sister Siby became insistent. He remembered the day she had been taken by those monsters, a distant memory, tormenting him, few hopes remained within him, not recognizing himself after all those he managed to fix, often the circumstances in which he lived. He found a glimmer of hope, in that light, which a few hours earlier had managed to drive those monsters away, had done what he, in all that time, had been unable to make a decision, failing.

He asked himself why he hadn't been so lucky to find something similar. His anger consumed him.

The boys had already consumed part of their supplies. Some of them were resting, others were standing guard in front of the shelter. Ten couldn't sleep; his worry was immense; he couldn't explain how a simple flash of light could have driven such creatures away. He remembered the times when he'd ventured out alone looking for answers. When Tesk and Sid's turn came to stand guard, Ten was still awake. His hand was searching for the tip of the spear, trying to understand the secret of its strength.

He stood up and left the shelter. The commander was resting. The cold of the forest entered the shelter and made the boys shiver. The fire was their only source of light; the little light that did enter illuminated part of their hiding place.

Ten reached the fire and knelt down. He tried to clear his thoughts. He couldn't remember anyone ever mentioning that strange light before.

Steph woke up to take part in the guard shift. As the two of them returned to the shelter, she approached Ten.

"What's wrong? Can't you sleep?"

Ten, keeping his gaze fixed on the fire, replied.

"We're on guard."

The wind stirred the flames. Steph sat down next to him, but his companion wasn't in the mood to talk, so he didn't turn around, trapped in his thoughts.

"What happened in the forest today?" he asked.

Ten didn't answer at first, his mind still preoccupied, and he only understood the question a few seconds later.

"We've been searching for answers for years, and it all happened in a matter of seconds."

"What did you see? Why were those monsters scared?"

Ten looked at Steph. He hadn't often heard him ask two questions in a row in the last few years.

Ten looked at Steph. He hadn't often heard him ask two questions in a row in the last few years.

"Today I came across things I hadn't seen in years. None of us knew there was anything to keep them away. A simple light chased those monsters away."

Steph sensed she'd found something.

"The light, where did it come from?"

Ten continued to stare into the fire, overcome with frustration, searching for answers no one could give her. She opened the bag with only her left hand and rummaged around without looking back. After finding the spearhead, she showed it to him. Steph looked at it for a moment. It was a simple spearhead, similar to the ones he made for the rest of the search party. He picked it up.

"Did this drive those things away?"

Ten looked back at the fire, his face expressing resignation. Steph doubted he knew the nature of the stone. The danger he had faced as a boy had led him to risk his life, and he was more than aware of it. His resignation turned to fear.

The village guards scoured every corner for Victor. Some helped the elders return and bring them oil for their lamps to light at night, making sure they had enough supplies. Soc and another guard headed to Gressy. They needed to ask her some questions. Soc knew the woman was hiding something that could help them understand what was happening.

Riz saw them from afar and called out to them.

"Soc, where are you going? What will we do while we wait?"

Soc knew something was threatening the village. He remembered what he'd seen before, even though he'd never told anyone. He knew Gressy could help them. They needed to find out what had happened to Victor.

"Let's go to Gressy! Riz, make sure everyone in the village has hair."

"Soc!"

Soc and the guard walked a few hundred meters before turning the corner onto Gressy's street.

When they arrived, they noticed the door wide open, so they quickened their pace. Smoke was pouring from the house. They thought he might have left the house and started the fire. They found Vincent trying to put out the flames, and immediately asked him,

"Where's Gressy?"

Vincent turned to look at them.

"He's in there. With Joseph."

The two approached the bedroom.

"Gressy, we need to talk to you."

The woman was tucking Joseph into bed, still not fully awake.

"Yes, tell me," she replied, leaving the room.

They turned toward the dining table as they moved.

"Gressy, we know something's wrong. When was the last time you saw Victor?"

Gressy continued walking toward the fire. Vincent was there.

"Gressy!" Soc repeated.

"Victor was with Joseph. When I came back, he was gone."

"Do you know anything? We need to wake Joseph."

Gressy continued to fix the fire, in a hurry. Smoke was pouring out of the door. She looked at Vincent.

"Move away."

Soc knew she had been involved in many things in the past that no one could explain. A woman like that understood some of the knowledge needed to ward off danger. Smoke was pouring out of the house, rising into the sky. From afar, the trail it left could be seen above the roof. Soc ordered the other guard to go out and make sure no one approached.

Soc remembered that a long time ago, someone had seen Gressy emerge from behind a moving tree.

No one had believed what they had seen, blaming her for scaring the village.

Soc asked her again,

"Gressy, we know what you've been hiding all these years, and no one ever blamed you for how you helped the village. Is what happened in the past happening again?"

Joseph's over there. I don't know what's happening to him."

Soc snorted. He looked out the door for a moment.

If you can tell me what we're going through, I can save more people."

The situation in the village was new. Since the time when darkness had dominated that land, no one remembered having experienced similar situations, nor did they remember the size of the creatures that had frightened the inhabitants. Gressy was planning something, and Soc sensed she was hiding something from him.

"Listen!" the woman shouted.

"Joseph's in there. He's asleep. And I don't know why he's like that."

Soc looked her in the eye and immediately left the house, ordering the guard to fetch some herbal oil for the lamp. Gessi searched the house for something, so he turned to look at Vincent, who was staring at the fire. Gressy noticed that the flame had changed color. She moved closer for a moment.

"Vincent! Come here!"

The boy approached her, from across the table. Gressy shifted her gaze to the dresser drawer. She approached and opened it. She began rummaging but found nothing. Only objects she knew she'd put there. Gressy turned to Vincent. She immediately went to Joseph's room to check on him. But she found him there, lying on the bed. She returned to the fire, which had stopped changing color. Vincent remained, looking over the threshold. Soc reentered the house, passing Vincent, who, a few meters away, was staring outside.

He went to Gressy, who was in Joseph's room.

"Gressy! You'll spend the night safe here. We'll be back later. The other guard is bringing you some herbal oil for the candlelight."

Gressy didn't pay much attention, continuing to check on Joseph. He grabbed her arm, saying,

"Did you hear?"

The woman nodded.

Soc rushed to the exit and found Vincent there, who remained where he was.

"Boy, close the door and fix that fire."

Then he went to meet the guard, who was arriving with the oil.

"Keep an eye on them, there's something going on in there."

"Will I have to stay here for the night?"

"You'll keep watch for a while, then join us."

The man nodded. Soc headed toward the center of the village, joining the other guards. Night was falling as oil lamps were placed in front of each house. The windows of the houses were all shut. In the village, only the lamps could be seen, illuminating the streets. The center of the square was empty; the guards didn't know what to expect.

"Did you give the people what they needed?" Soc asked.

One of the guards spoke up.

"Yes. I tried to enter one house, but the door was locked."

"Take me there. You two stay here. Spread out in groups of two across the village."

"Take me there, quickly!"

Soc and the guard ran toward the house. There seemed to be no movement, and no sound coming from inside. So they tried to force the door open. His companion pushed, while Soc grabbed the spear from behind and began shouting, pounding the door.

"Is there anyone inside?!"

They heard the sound of breaking glass coming from behind the house. Soc rushed to the back, where a small window had shattered. He immediately realized it wasn't a person who had escaped; he could never have gotten through there. He returned to the front of the house. The guard, meanwhile, had managed to open the door. Inside, he found an old woman lying on the floor, her eyes grayish. Soc rushed inside to check if anyone was in the other rooms. The guard searched the rest of the house. When they returned, the old woman was no longer there; it was as if someone had taken her away. Soc looked at the guard.

"But where did she go? Wasn't she here?"

Meanwhile, dark drops began to fall from the ceiling of the room.

Soc bent down, touching them with his fingers, then rubbed them. He quickly got up and walked out the door.

"What are they?" asked the other guard.

"Let's go," he replied.

"Are we in danger? What's going on?"

As they headed into the square, movement on a rooftop caught their attention. Soc was a few meters ahead and began shouting,

"Who's there?"

As their attention swung, Soc sensed something moving beyond his vision.

He took a few steps forward and shouted to the other guard,

"Can you see anything?"

The other guard didn't respond, as Soc continued to get closer and closer. Another window pane shattered a little further away. He turned to his companion, who was petrified. He reached her. Her eyes were grayish. She began to scream; the other guards could hear her screams.

Soc tried to shake the man, but he didn't make any sign. Meanwhile, more screams rose from another house.

Soc turned in the direction of the screams. A moment later, he turned back, but the guard had disappeared. He could see liquid at his feet. His companions were reaching him. Instinctively, he looked up to see that he was getting closer. He looked back at the ground, but the liquid had disappeared.

"Soc, what's going on? Where's the other guard?" the guards asked him.

"Go check the house nearby. Someone's in danger."

Gressy continued trying to tidy up the house. The fire gave her a signal she didn't immediately perceive.

Meanwhile, drops of rain began to drip from the ceiling. Gressy didn't notice; she continued searching for the object in the drawer.

She asked Vincent if he had seen it. Vincent didn't answer. Joseph continued to sleep. The woman began filling bags. She couldn't stay still; her mind was restless. Vincent approached the fire. For a moment, the smoke stopped clouding the house. Gressy paused for a moment to clear her thoughts, to ask herself what she could do and where to go.

Joseph made strange sounds. The woman ran to him to see what was happening and called his name repeatedly. When she heard no response, she turned to Vincent. She felt Joseph stirring and approached to check on him. At that moment, she could see that he was wet. She returned to Vincent, who was staring at the fire, which changed color again. Something was beginning to torment Gressy's mind. She looked at the fire, ordering Vincent to move away. He obeyed, and Gressy noticed strange drops falling to the floor. As she turned, something passed behind the window; near the fire, she could only see its shadow. Gressy grabbed the bags and asked Vincent to go to Joseph's room. She added wood to the fire. She turned around and saw drops falling from the ceiling. Smoke began to fill the entire house.

Gressy reached Joseph's room. She took Vincent and Joseph with her and went out. Something broke Joseph's bedroom window. As they walked away toward the lake, something erupted inside the house. The house was gripped by an illness. Gressy was the only one who could hear the din that had permeated the walls. They ran toward the lake, which was only a few hundred meters from her house. She asked Vincent to move. The body of water was now close. Something was following them. The woman noticed the movement and headed to her right, where the stream marked the safe zone bordering the village. As she changed direction, she heard something scuffing inside Joseph's pocket. She couldn't stop, but she could guess what he might have in his pocket. Something was following them, making sounds similar to those Joseph had made at the lake. The sound alone made the child's eyes widen. Looking back, she could see a creature with long ears stalking them.

They were almost near the stream; Gressy knew that crossing it would mean crossing one of the boundaries. Then they would find the one with the candles. The shouts coming from the village disturbed her; she turned to look at her house and the rest of the town. But something caught her attention: a being barely a meter tall was behind them, moving very slowly. Gressy stopped to look at it, while the strange animal asked her,

"Do you remember when you came out of the tree, Gressy?"

Her eyes widened, gorging.

The woman began rummaging through Joseph's pocket. Vincent hid behind her.

"Where's Joseph?"

"You'll all be caught. But you have something we need."

Gressy grabbed the object and blew into it, making the creature disappear. They turned and ran across the stream.

Meanwhile, in the village, the guards were searching every corner. Some lanterns in front of the houses were out, and out of concern, they knocked on every single door to make sure everyone was safe. Some people had disappeared. They couldn't figure out what entity had targeted the village, nor could they try to stop it. Soc continued searching every corner of the village, searching for the strange liquid, while his companions visited every house that had been targeted. The situation was out of control. But Soc remembered Gressy's house. He turned and noticed the smoke coming from it. He realized it was the only house sending those signals. The strange beings disappeared from the village. Soc ordered his men to gather in the center of the square, ordering his men to stay there. A few moments later, he headed for Gressy's house. He knew something was wrong; he could see fog approaching from the lake. He turned toward Gressy's house and began running toward her. As he got closer, the fog on the lake disappeared. When he reached the house, he saw the door was wide open and thick smoke was coming out of it. The strange liquid was all over the floor of the house.